Vicky Van

By Carolyn Wells

Originally published in 1918

Vicky Van

Published by Resurrected Press

This classic book was handcrafted by Resurrected Press. Resurrected Press is dedicated to bringing high quality classic books back to the readers who enjoy them. These are not scanned versions of the originals, but, rather, quality checked and edited books meant to be enjoyed!

Please visit ResurrectedPress.com to view our entire catalogue!

ISBN 13: 978-1-937022-04-4

Printed in the United States of America

OTHER RESURRECTED PRESS MYSTERIES

By Louis Tracy
The Strange Case of Mortimer Fenley
The Albert Gate Mystery
The Stowmarket Mystery

By J. S. Fletcher
The Orange-Yellow Diamond
The Middle Temple Murder
Scarhaven Keep
Ravensdene Court

By A. A. Milne
The Red House Mystery

By Agatha Christie
The Mysterious Affair at Styles

By Arthur Griffiths
The Passenger from Calais
The Rome Express

From the Dr. John Thorndyke Series
By R. Austin Freeman
The Red Thumb Mark
The Eye of Osiris
The Mystery of 31 New Inn
John Thorndyke's Cases
A Silent Witness
The Cat's Eye

By Arthur J. Rees
The Hampstead Mystery
The Mystery of the Downs
The Shrieking Pit
The Hand in The Dark
The Moon Rock

Visit RessurectedPress.com to see our entire catalog.

FOREWORD

Carolyn Wells was one of a group of American women authors, who at the end of the nineteenth and into the beginning of the twentieth century took the mystery along a new and different path. Set in the domestic world of the newly prominent middle and professional class then arising in the urban areas, their mysteries had less to do with violence and greed and more to do with the relationships between people.

Vicky Van deals with the collision of two adjacent but very different worlds, the Fifth Avenue world of old money, image, and position as exemplified by the victim, Randolph Schuyler, and the "Just off Fifth Avenue" world of middle class lawyers and professional men as typified by the narrator of the story, the young lawyer, Chester Calhoun. The mysterious Victoria Van Allen, the "Vicky Van" of the title occupies a curious position in between, a young woman of independent means, excellent taste, and faultless fashion sense but no known antecedents. Known for her charity work and bridge parties she is acceptable, but not quite respectable.

Published in 1918 the story is set in a vaguely pre-World War I New York. There are telephones and cars, but the style and manners are still pre-war. Class is still important, and even the up and coming members of the middle class realize that they are not on the top of the heap. The horde of immigrants flooding through Ellis Island were destined to be waiters and servants and other such menials.

Though a mystery, and involving a murder, the story is much more a comment on the collision between the worlds of Fifth Avenue and just off Fifth Avenue, how the various participants view their roles and the two worlds. Detection, is in many ways an afterthought. The professional detective, Fleming Stone doesn't make an appearance until two thirds of the way through the book, and most of the real investigation is handled by his youthful assistant, Fisby. There is no elaborate trail of clues or misleading red herrings, the solution in the end is improbable at best. What is important is the relationships between Calhoun and Vicky Van and Ruth Schuyler.

Wells was a prolific writer, with some 170 books published, with more than half of them being mysteries. Though not as well known today as some others, her writing gives a glance into a world now gone. Resurrected Press is happy to offer you this new edition of *Vicky Van*.

About the Author

Carolyn Wells, June 18, 1862 - March 26, 1942 was an American writer and poet. She was best known for her books of poetry and humor until around 1910 she read one of Anna Katherine Green's mysteries and took up the genre. Many of her mysteries featured the detective Fleming Stone. She was married to Hadwin Houghton, heir to the Houghton-Mifflin publishing company. She was a collector of poetry by other authors, and, upon her death, she bequeathed her collection of the works of Walt Witman to the Library of Congress.

Greg Fowlkes
Editor-In-Chief
Resurrected Press
www.ResurrectedPress.com

TABLE OF CONTENTS

CHAPTER 1: VICKY VAN

Victoria Van Allen was the name she signed to her letters and to her cheques, but Vicky Van, as her friends called her, was signed all over her captivating personality, from the top of her dainty, tossing head to the tips of her dainty, dancing feet.

I liked her from the first, and if her "small and earlies" were said to be so called because they were timed by the small and early numerals on the clock dial, and if her "little" bridge games kept in active circulation a goodly share of our country's legal tender, those things are not crimes.

I lived in one of the polite sections of New York City, up among the East Sixties, and at the insistence of my sister and aunt, who lived with me, our home was near enough the great boulevard to be designated by that enviable phrase, "Just off Fifth Avenue." We were on the north side of the street, and, nearer to the Avenue, on the south side, was the home of Vicky Van.

Before I knew the girl, I saw her a few times, at long intervals, on the steps of her house, or entering her little car, and half-consciously I noted her charm and her evident zest of life.

Later, when a club friend offered to take me there to call, I accepted gladly, and as I have said, I liked her from the first.

And yet, I never said much about her to my sister. I am, in a way, responsible for Winnie, and too, she's too young to go where they play Bridge for money. Little faddly prize bags or gift-shop novelties are her stakes.

Also, Aunt Lucy, who helps me look after Win, wouldn't quite understand the atmosphere at Vicky's. Not exactly Bohemian—and yet, I suppose it did represent one compartment of that handy-box of a term. But I'm going to tell you, right now, about a party I went to there, and you can see for yourself what Vicky Van was like.

"How late you're going out," said Winnie, as I slithered into my topcoat. "It's after eleven."

"Little girls mustn't make comments on big brothers," I smiled back at her. Win was nineteen and I had attained the mature age of twenty-seven. We were orphans and spinster Aunt Lucy did her best to be a parent to us; and we got on smoothly enough, for none of us had the temperament that rouses friction in the home.

"Across the street?" Aunt Lucy guessed, raising her aristocratic eyebrows a hair's breadth.

"Yes," I returned, the least bit irritated at the implication of that hairbreadth raise. "Steele will be over there and I want to see him—"

This time the said eyebrows went up frankly in amusement, and the kind blue eyes beamed as she said, "All right, Chet, run along."

Though I was Chester Calhoun, the junior partner of the law firm of Bradbury and Calhoun, and held myself in due and consequent respect, I didn't mind Aunt Lucy's calling me Chet, or even, as she sometimes did, Chetty. A man puts up with those things from the women of his household. As to Winnie, she called me anything that came handy, from Lord Chesterton to Chessy-Cat.

I patted Aunt Lucy on her soft old shoulder and Winnie on her hard young head, and was off.

True, I did expect to see Steele at Vicky Van's—he was the club chap who had introduced me there—but as Aunt Lucy had so cleverly suspected, he was not my sole reason for going. A bigger reason was that I always had a good time there, the sort of a good time I liked.

I crossed the street diagonally, in defiance of much good advice I have heard and read against such a proceeding. But at eleven o'clock at night the traffic in those upper side streets is not sufficient to endanger life or limb, and I reached Vicky Van's house in safety.

It was a very small house, and it was the one nearest to the Fifth Avenue corner, though the long side of the first house on that block of the Avenue lay between.

The windows on each floor were brilliantly lighted, and I mounted the long flight of stone steps sure of a merry welcome and a jolly time.

I was admitted by a maid whom I already knew well enough to say "Evening, Julie," as I passed her, and in another moment, I was in the long, narrow living-room and was a part of the gay group there.

"Angel child!" exclaimed Vicky Van herself, dancing toward me, "did he come to see his little ole friend?" and laying her two hands in mine for an instant, she considered me sufficiently welcomed, and danced off again. She was a will o' the wisp, always tantalizing a man with a hope of special attention, and then flying away to another guest, only to treat him in the same way.

I looked after her, a slim, graceful thing, vibrant with the joy of living, smiling in sheer gayety of heart, and pretty as a picture.

Her black hair was arranged in the newest style, that covered her ears with soft loops and exposed the shape of her trim little head. It was banded with a jeweled fillet, or whatever they call those Oriental things they wear, and her big eyes with their long, dark lashes, her pink cheeks and curved scarlet lips seemed to say, "the world owes me a living and I'm going to collect."

Not as a matter of financial obligation, be it understood.

Vicky Van had money enough and though nothing about her home was ostentatious or over ornate, it was quietly and in the best of taste luxurious.

But I was describing Vicky herself. Her gown, the skirt part of it, was a sort of mazy maize-colored thin stuff, rather short and rather full, that swirled as she moved, and fluttered when she danced. The bodice part, was of heavily gold-spangled material, and a kind of overskirt arrangement was a lot of long gold fringe made of beads. Instead of a yoke, there were shoulder straps of these same beads, and the sleeves weren't there.

And yet, that costume was all right. Why, it was a rig I'd be glad to see Winnie in, when she gets older, and if I've made it sound rather—er—gay and festive, it's my bungling way of describing it, and also, because Vicky's personality would add gayety and festivity to any raiment.

Her little feet wore goldy slippers, and a lot of ribbons criss-crossed over her ankles, and on the top of each slipper was a gilt butterfly that fluttered.

Yet with all this bewildering effect of frivolity, the first term I'd make use of in describing Vick's character would be Touch-me-not. I believe there's a flower called that—noli me tangere—or some such name. Well, that's Vicky Van. She'd laugh and jest with you, and then if you said anything by way of a personal compliment or flirtatious foolery, she was off and away from your side, like a thistle-down in a summer breeze. She was a witch, a madcap, but she had her own way in everything, and her friends did her will without question.

Her setting, too, just suited her. Her living room was one of those very narrow, very deep rooms so often seen in the New York side streets. It was done up in French gray and rose, as was the dictum of the moment. On the rose-brocaded walls were few pictures, but just the right ones. Gray enameled furniture and deep window-seats with rose-colored cushions provided resting-places, and soft rose-shaded lights gave a mild glow of illumination.

Flowers were everywhere. Great bowls of roses, jars of pink carnations and occasionally a vase of pink orchids were on mantel, low bookcases or piano. And sometimes the odor of a cigarette or a burning pastille of Oriental fragrance, added to the Bohemian effect which is, oftener than not, discernible by the sense of smell.

Vicky herself, detested perfumes or odors of any kind, save fresh flowers all about. Indeed, she detested Bohemianism, when it meant unconventional dress or manners or loud-voiced jests or songs.

Her house was dainty, correct and artistic, and yet, I knew its atmosphere would not please my Aunt Lucy, or be just the right place for Winnie.

Many of the guests I knew. Cassie Weldon was a concert singer and Ariadne Gale an artist of some prominence, both socially and in her art circle. Jim Ferris and Bailey Mason were actors of a good sort, and Bert Garrison, a member of one of my best clubs, was a fast rising architect. Steele hadn't come yet.

Two tables of bridge were playing in the back part of the room, and in the rest of the rather limited space several couples were dancing.

"Mayn't we open the doors to the dining room, Vicky?" called out one of the card players. "The calorics of this room must be about ninety in the shade."

"Open them a little way," returned Miss Van Allen. "But not wide, for there's a surprise supper and I don't want you to see it yet."

They set the double doors a few inches ajar and went on with their game. The dining room, as I knew, was a wide room that ran all across the house behind both living-room and hall. It was beautifully decorated in pale green and silver, and often Vicky Van would have a "surprise supper," at which the favors or entertainers would be well worth waiting for.

Having greeted many whom I knew, I looked about for further speech with my hostess.

"She's upstairs in the music room," said Cassie Weldon, seeing and interpreting my questing glance.

"Thank you, lady, for those kind words," I called back over my shoulder, and went upstairs.

The front room on the second floor was dubbed the "music room," Vicky said, because there was a banjo in it.

Sometimes the guests brought more banjos and a concert of glees and college songs would ensue. But more often, as to-night, it was a little haven of rest and peace from the laughter and jest below stairs.

It was an exquisite white and gold room, and here, too, as I entered, pale pink shades dimmed the lights to a soft radiance that seemed like a breaking dawn.

Vicky sat enthroned on a white divan, her feet crossed on a gold-embroidered white satin foot-cushion. In front of her sat three or four of her guests all laughing and chatting.

"But he vowed he was going to get here somehow," Mrs. Reeves was saying.

"What's his name?" asked Vicky, though in a voice of little interest.

"Somers," returned Mrs. Reeves.

"Never heard of him. Did you, Mr. Calhoun?" and Vicky Van looked up at me as I entered.

"No; Miss Van Allen. Who is he?"

"I don't know and I don't care. Only as Mrs. Reeves says he is coming here tonight, I'd like to know something about him."

"Coming here! A man you don't know?" I drew up a chair to join the group. "How can he?"

"Mr. Steele is going to bring him," said Mrs. Reeves. "He says—Norman Steele says, that Mr. Somers is a first-class all-around chap, and no end of fun. Says he's a millionaire."

"What's a millionaire more or less to me?" laughed Vicky. "I choose my friends for their lovely character, not for their wealth."

"Yes, you've selected all of us for that, dear," agreed Mrs. Reeves, "but this Somers gentleman may be amiable, too."

Mrs. Reeves was a solid, sensible sort of person, who acted as ballast for the volatile Vicky, and sometimes reprimanded her in a mild way.

"I love the child," she had said to me once, "and she is a little brick. But once in a while I have to tell her a few things for the good of the community. She takes it all like an angel."

"Well, I don't care," Vicky went on, "Norman Steele has no right to bring anybody here whom he hasn't asked me about. If I don't like him, I shall ask some of you nice, amiable men to get me a long plank, and we'll put it out of a window, and make him walk it. Shall we?"

We all agreed to do this, or to tar and feather and ride on a rail any gentleman who might in any way be so unfortunate as to fall one iota short of Vicky Van's requirements.

"And now," said Vicky, "if you'll all please go downstairs, except Mrs. Reeves and Mr. Garrison and my own sweet self, I'll be orfly obliged to you."

The sweeping gesture with which she sought to dismiss us was a wave of her white arms and a smile of her red lips, and I, for one, found it impossible to obey. I started with the rest, and then after the gay crowd were part way down stairs I turned back.

"Please, mayn't I join your little class, if I'll be very good?" I begged. "I don't want Bert Garrison to be left alone at the mercy of two such sirens."

Miss Van Allen hesitated. Her pink-tipped forefinger rested a moment on her curved lip. "Yes," she said, nodding her head. "Yes, stay, Mr. Calhoun. You may be a help. Are you any good at getting theatre boxes after they're all sold?"

"That's my profession," I returned. "I learned it from a correspondence school. Where's the theatre? Lead me to it!"

"It's the Metropolis Theatre," she replied. "And I want to have a party there to-morrow night, and I want two boxes, and this awful, dreadful, bad Mr. Garrison says they're all sold, and I can't get any! What can you do about it?"

"Oh, I'll fix it. I'll go to the people who bought the boxes you want, and—I don't know what I'll say to them, exactly—but I'll fix up such a yarn that they'll beg me to take the boxes off their hands."

"Oh, will you, really?" and the dazzling smile she gave me would have repaid a much greater Herculean task than I had undertaken. And, of course, I hadn't meant it, but when she thought I did, I couldn't go back on my word.

"I'll do my best, Miss Van Allen," I said, seriously, "and if I can't possibly turn the trick, I'll—well, I'll buy the Metropolitan Opera House, and put on a show of my own."

"No," she laughed, "you needn't do that. But if you try and fail—why, we'll just have a little party here, a sort of consolation party, and—oh, let's have some private theatricals. Wouldn't that be fun!"

"More fun than the original program?" I asked quickly, hoping to be let off my promise.

"No, sir!" she cried, "decidedly not! I want especially to have that theatre party and supper afterward at the Britz. Now you do all you can, won't you?"

I promised to do all I could, and I had a partial hope I could get what she wanted by hook or crook, and then, as she heard a specially favorite fox-trot being dashed off on the piano downstairs, she sprang from her seat, and kicking the satin cushion aside, asked me to dance. In a moment we were whirling around the music room to the zipping music, and Mrs. Reeve and Garrison followed in our steps.

Vicky danced with a natural born talent that is quite unlike anything acquired by lessons. I had no need to guide her, she divined my lead, and swayed in any direction, even as I was about to indicate it. I had never danced with anyone who danced so well, and I was profuse in my thanks and praise.

"I love it," she said simply, as she patted the gold fringes of her gown into place. "I adore dancing, and you are one of the best partners I have ever had. Come, let us go down and cut into a Bridge game. We'll just about have time before supper."

Pirouetting before me, she led the way, and we went down the long steep stairs.

A shout greeted her appearance in the doorway.

"Oh, Vicky, we have missed you! Come over here and listen to Ted's latest old joke!"

"No, come over here and hear this awful gossip Ariadne is telling for solemn truth. It's the very worst taradiddle she ever got off!"

"Here's a place, Vicky Van, a nice cosy corner, 'tween Jim and me. Come on, Ladygirl."

"No, thanks, everybody. I'm going to cut in at this table. May I? Am I a nuisance?"

"A Vicky-nuisance! They ain't no such animal!" and Bailey Mason rose to give her his chair.

"No," said she, "I want you to stay, Mr. Mason. 'Cause why, I want to play wiz you. Cassie, you give me your place, won't you, Ducky-Daddles? and you go and flirt with Mr. Calhoun. He knows the very newest flirts! Go, give him a tryout."

Vicky Van settled herself into her seat with the happy little sigh of the bridge lover, who sits down with three good players, and in another moment she was breathlessly looking over her hand. "Without," she said, triumphantly, and knowing she'd say no word more to me for the present, I walked away with Cassie Weldon.

And Cassie was good fun. She took me to the piano, and with the soft pedal down, she showed me a new little tone picture she had made up, which was both picturesque and funny.

"You'd better go into vaudeville!" I exclaimed, as she finished, "your talent is wasted on the concert platform."

"That's what Vicky tells me," she returned. "Sometimes I believe I will try it, just for fun."

"You'll find it such fun, you'll stay in for earnest," I assured her, for she had shown a bit of inventive genius that I felt sure would make good in a little musical turn.

CHAPTER 2: MR. SOMERS

It was nearly midnight when Steele came, and with him was a man I had never seen before, and whom I assumed to be the Mr. Somers I had heard about.

And it was. As Steele entered, he cast his eye around for Vicky, and saw her at the bridge table down at the end of the room. Her back was toward us, and she was so absorbed in the game she did not look round, if, indeed, she heard the noise of their arrival.

The two men stopped near the group I was with and Steele introduced Mr. Somers.

A little curiously I looked at him, and saw a large, self-satisfied looking man wearing an expansive smile and expensive apparel. Clothes the very best procurable, jewelry just inside the limits of good taste—he bore himself like a gentleman, yet there was an unmistakable air of ostentatious wealth that repelled me. A second look made me think Mr. Somers had dined either late or twice, but his greetings were courteous and genial and his manner sociable, if a little patronizing. He seemed a stranger to all present, and his eye roved about for the charming hostess Steele had told him of.

"We'll reach Miss Van Allen presently." Steele laughed, in answer to the glance, "if, indeed, we dare interrupt her game. Let's make progress slowly."

"No hurry," returned Somers, affably, beaming on Cassie Weldon and meeting Ariadne Gale's receptive smile. "I'm anchored here for the moment. Miss Weldon? Ah, yes, I've heard you sing. Voice like a lark—like a lark."

Clearly, Somers was not much of a purveyor of small talk. I sized him up for a lumbering oldster, who wanted to be playful but didn't quite know how.

He had rather an austere face, yet there was a gleam in his eye that belied the austerity. His cheeks were fat and red, his nose prominent, and he was clean shaven, save for a thick white mustache, that drooped slightly on either side of a full-lipped mouth. His hair was white, his eyes dark and deep-set, and he could easily be called a handsome man. He was surely fifty, and perhaps more. Had it not been for a certain effusiveness in his speech, I could have liked him, but he seemed to me to lack sincerity.

However, I am not one to judge harshly or hastily, and I met him half way, and even helped him in his efforts at gay affability.

"You've never been here before?" I asked; "Good old Steele to bring you to-night."

"No, never before," and he glanced around appreciatively, "but I shall, I hope, come often. Charming little nest; charming ladies!" a bow included those nearest.

"Yes, indeed," babbled Ariadne, "fair women and brave men."

"Brave, yes," agreed Somers, "to dare the glances of such bright eyes. I must protect my heart!" He clasped his fat hands pretty near where his heart was situated, and grinned with delight as Ariadne also "protected" her heart.

"Ah," he cried, "two hearts in danger! I feel sure we shall be friends, if only because misery loves company."

"Is it really misery with you?" and Ariadne's sympathy was so evidently profound, that Cassie Weldon and I walked away.

"I'll give Ariad her innings," said the vivacious Miss Weldon, "and I'll make up to the Somers kid later. Where'd Vicky pick him up?"

"She doesn't know him at all. Norman Steele brought him unbeknownst."

"No! Why, Vick doesn't allow that sort of thing."

"So I'm told. Any way, Steele did it."

"Well, Vicky's such a good-natured darling, maybe she won't mind for once. She won't, if she likes the little stranger. He's well-meaning, at any rate."

"So's Ariadne. From her smile, I think she well means to sell him her latest 'Autumn In The Adirondacks,' or 'Lady With A Handbag'."

"Now, don't be mean!" but Cassie laughed. "And I don't blame her if she does. Poor Ad paints above the heads of the public, so if this is a high-up Publican, she'd better make sales while the sun shines."

"What's her work like?"

"You can see more of it in this house than anywhere else. Vicky is so fond of Ariadne and so sorry her pictures don't sell better, that she buys a lot herself."

"Does Miss Gale know Miss Van Allen does it out of—"

"Don't say charity! No, they're really good stuff, and Vicky buys 'em for Christmas gifts and bridge prizes."

"Does she ever play for prizes? I thought she liked a bit of a stake, now."

"Yes, at evening parties. But, often we have a dove game of an afternoon, with prizes and pink tea. Vicky Van isn't a gay doll, you know. She's—sometimes, she's positively domestic. I wish she had a nice husband and some little kiddies."

"Why hasn't she?"

"Give it up. She's never seen any man she loved, I s'pose."

"Perhaps she'll love this Somers person."

"Heaven forbid! Nothing less than a crown prince would suit Vicky Van. Look, she's turning to meet him. Won't he be bowled over!"

I turned, and though there were several people between us, I caught a glimpse of Somers' face as he was presented to Miss Van Allen. He was bowled over. His eyes beamed with admiration and he bowed low as he raised to his lips the dainty, bejeweled hand.

Vicky, apparently, did not welcome this old-time greeting, and she drew away her hand, saying, "not allowed. Naughty man! Express proper compunction, or you can't sit next me at supper!"

"Forgive me," begged Somers. "I'm sorry! I'll never do it again—until after I sit next you at supper!"

"More brains than I thought," I said to Cassie, who nodded, and then Vicky Van rose from her chair.

"Take my place for a moment, Mr. Somers," she said, standing before him. "I—" she dropped her eyes adorably, "I must see about the arrangement of seats at the supper table." With a merry laugh, she ran from the room, and through the long hall to the dining-room.

Somers dropped into her vacant chair, and continued the Bridge game with the air of one who knows how to play.

In less than five minutes Vicky was back. "No, keep the hand," she said, as he rose. "I've played long enough. And supper will be ready shortly."

"Finish the rubber,—I insist" Somers returned, and as he determinedly stood behind the chair, Vicky, perforce, sat down.

He continued to stand behind her chair, watching her play. Vicky was too sure of her game to be rattled at his close scrutiny, but it seemed to me her shoulders shrugged a little impatiently, as he criticized or commended her plays.

She had thrown a light scarf of gauze or tulle around when she was out of the room, and being the same color as her gown, it made her seem more than ever like an houri. She smiled up into Somers' face, and then, coyly, her long lashes fell on her pink cheeks. Evidently, she had concluded to bewitch the newcomer, and she was making good.

I drew nearer, principally because I liked to look at her. She was a live wire to-night! She looked roguish, and she made most brilliant plays, tossing down her cards with gay little gestures, and doing trick shuffles with her twinkling fingers.

"You could have had that last trick, if you'd played for it," Somers said, as the rubber finished.

"I know it," Vicky conceded. "I saw, just too late, that I was getting the lead into the wrong hand."

"Well, don't ever do that again," he said, lightly, "never again."

As he said the last word, he laid his finger tips on her shoulder. It was the veriest touch, the shoulder was swathed in the transparent tulle, but still, it roused Vicky. She glanced up at him, and I looked at him, too. But Somers was not in flirtatious mood. He said, "I beg your pardon," in most correct fashion. Had he then, touched her inadvertently? It didn't seem so, but his speech assured it.

Vicky jumped up from the table, and ignoring Somers, ran out to the hall, saying something about looking after the surprise for the supper. To my surprise, Somers followed her, not hastily, but rather deliberately, and, quelling an absurd impulse to go, too, I turned to Norman Steele, who stood near.

"Who's this Somers?" I asked him, rather abruptly. "Is he all right?"

"You bet," said Steele, smiling. "He's a top-notcher."

"In what respects?"

"Every and all."

"You've known him long?"

"Yes. I tell you Cal, he's all right. Forget it. What's the surprise for supper? Do you know?"

"Of course not. It wouldn't be a surprise if we all knew of it."

"Well, Vicky's surprises are always great fun. Why the grouch, old man? Can't you chirrup?"

"Oh, I'm all right," and I felt annoyed that he read in my face that I was put out. But I didn't like the looks of

Somers, and I couldn't say so to the man who had brought him there.

"Oh, please! Oh, please!" shouted a hoarse, strange voice, and one scarcely to be heard above the hum of gay voices and peals of gay laughter, "oh, somebody, please!"

I looked across the room, and in the wide hall doorway stood a man, who was quite evidently a waiter. He was white-faced and staring-eyed, and he fairly hung on to a portiere for support, as he repeated his agonized plea.

"What is it?" said Mrs. Reeves, as everybody else stared at the man. "What do you want?" She stepped toward him, and we all turned to look.

"Not you—no, Madame. Some man, please—some doctor. Is there one here?"

"Some of the servants ill?" asked Mrs. Reeves, kindly. "Doctor Remson, will you come?"

The pleasant-faced capable-looking woman paused only until Doctor Remson joined her, and the two went into the hall, the waiter following slowly.

In a moment I heard a shriek, a wild scream. Partly curiosity and partly a foreboding of harm to Vicky Van, made me rush forward.

Mrs. Reeves had screamed, and I ran the length of the hall to the dining room. There I saw Somers on the floor, and Remson bending over him.

"He's killed! He's stabbed!" cried Mrs. Reeves, clutching at my arm as I reached her. "Oh, what shall we do?"

She stood just in the dining-room doorway, which was at the end of the long hall, as in most city houses. The room was but dimly lighted, the table candles not yet burning.

"Keep the people back!" I shouted, as those in the living-room pressed out into the hall. "Steele, keep those girls back!"

There was an awful commotion. The men urged the women back, but curiosity and horror made them surge forward in irresistible force.

"Shut the door," whispered Remson. "This man is dead. It's an awful situation. Shut that door!"

Somehow, I managed to get the door closed between the dining-room and hall. On the inside were Remson, Mrs. Reeves, who wouldn't budge, and myself. Outside in the hall was a crowd of hysterical women and frightened men.

"Are you sure?" I asked, in a low voice, going nearer to the doctor and looking at Somers' fast-glazing eyes.

"Sure. He was stabbed straight to the heart with— see—a small, sharp knife."

Her hands over her eyes, but peering through her fingers, Mrs. Reeves drew near. "Not really," she moaned. "Oh, not really dead! Can't we do anything for him?"

"No," said Remson, rising to his feet, from his kneeling position. "He's dead, I tell you. Who did it?"

"That waiter—" I began, and then stopped. Looking in from a door opposite the hall door, probably one that led to a butler's pantry or kitchen, were half a dozen white-faced waiters.

"Come in here," said Remson; "not all of you. Which is chief?"

"I am, sir," and a head waiter came into the room. "What has happened?"

"A man has been killed," said the doctor, shortly. "Who are you? Who are you all? House servants?"

"No sir," said the chief. "We're caterer's men. From Fraschini's. I'm Luigi. We are here to serve supper."

"What do you know of this?"

"Nothing, sir," and the Italian looked truthful, though scared.

"Haven't you been in and out of the dining-room all evening?"

"Yes, sir. Setting the table, and such. But now it's all ready, and I was waiting Miss Van Allen's word to serve it."

"Where is Miss Van Allen?" I broke in.

"I—I don't know, sir," Luigi hesitated, and Doctor Remson interrupted.

"We mustn't ask these questions, Mr. Calhoun. We must call the police."

"The police!" cried Mrs. Reeves, "oh no! no! don't do that."

"It is my duty," said the doctor, firmly. "And no one must enter or leave this room until an officer arrives. You waiters, stay there in that pantry. Close those doors to the other room, Mr. Calhoun, please. Mrs. Reeves, I'm sorry, but I must ask you to stay here—"

"I won't do it!" declared the lady. "You're not an officer of the law. I'll stay in the house, but not in this room."

She stalked out into the hall, and Doctor Remson went at once to the telephone and called up headquarters.

The guests in the living room, hearing this, flew into a panic.

Of course, it was no longer possible, nor, as I could see, desirable to keep them in ignorance of what had happened.

After calling the police, Doctor Remson returned to his post just inside the dining-room door. He answered questions patiently, at first, but after being nearly driven crazy by the frantic women, he said, sharply, "You may all do just as you like. I've no authority here, except that the ethics of my profession dictate. That does not extend to jurisdiction over the guests present. But I advise you as a matter of common decency to stay here until this affair is investigated."

But they didn't. Many of them hastily gathered up their wraps and went out of the house as quickly as possible.

Cassie Weldon came to me in her distress.

"I must go, Mr. Calhoun," she said. "Don't you think I may? Why, it would interfere greatly with my work to have it known that I was mixed up in a—"

"You're not mixed up in it, Miss Weldon." I began to speak a little sternly, but the look in her eyes aroused my sympathy. "Well, go on," I said, "I suppose you will testify if called on. Everybody knows where to find you."

"Yes," she said, slowly, "but I hope I won't be called on. Why, it might spoil my whole career."

She slipped out of the door, in the wake of some other departing guests. After all, I thought, it couldn't matter much. Few, if any, of them were implicated, and they could all be found at their homes.

And yet, I had a vague idea that we ought all to stay.

"I shall remain and face the music," I heard Mrs. Reeves saying. "Where is Vicky? Do you suppose she knows about this? I'm going up in the music room to see if she's there. You know, with all the excitement down here, those upstairs may know nothing of it."

"I shall remain, too" said Ariadne Gale. "Why should anyone kill Mr. Somers? Did the caterer's people do it? What an awful thing! Will it be in the papers?"

"Will it!" said Garrison, who was standing near. "Reporters may be here any minute. Must be here as soon as the police come. Where is Miss Van Allen?"

"I don't know," and Ariadne began to cry.

"Stop that," said Mrs. Reeves, gruffly, but not unkindly. "Stay if you want to, Ariadne, but behave like a sensible woman, not a silly schoolgirl. This is an awful tragedy, of some sort."

"What do you mean, of some sort?" asked Miss Gale.

"I mean we don't know what revelations are yet to come. Where's Norman Steele? Where's the man who brought this Somers here?"

Sure enough, where was Steele? I had forgotten all about him. And it was he who had introduced Somers to the Van Allen house, and no one else present, so far as I knew, was previously acquainted with the man now lying dead the other side of that closed door.

I looked over the people who had stayed. Only a handful—perhaps half a dozen.

And then I wondered if I'd better go home myself. Not for my own sake, in any way; indeed, I preferred to remain, but I thought of Aunt Lucy and Win. Ought I to bring on them any shadow of trouble or opprobrium that might result from my presence in that house at that time? Would it not be better to go while I could do so? For, once the police took charge, I knew I should be called on to testify in public. And even as I debated with myself, the police arrived.

CHAPTER 3: THE WAITER'S STORY

Doctor Remson's police call had been imperative, and Inspector Mason came in with two men.

"What's this? What's wrong here?" the big burly inspector said, as he faced the few of us who had remained.

"Come in here, inspector," said the doctor, from the dining-room door.

And from that moment the whole aspect of the house seemed to change. No longer a gay little bijou residence, it became a court of justice.

One of the men was stationed at the street door and one at the area door below. Headquarters was notified of details. The coroner was summoned, and we were all for the moment under detention.

"Where is Miss Van Allen? Where is the lady of the house?" asked Mason. "Where are the servants? Who is in charge here?"

Was ever a string of questions so impossible of answers!

Doctor Remson told the main facts, but he was reticent. I, too, hesitated to say much, for the case was strange indeed.

Mrs. Reeves looked gravely concerned, but said nothing.

Ariadne Gale began to babble. That girl didn't know how to be quiet.

"I guess Miss Van Allen is upstairs," she volunteered. "She was in the dining-room, but she isn't here now, so she must be upstairs. Shall I go and see?"

"No!" thundered the inspector. "Stay where you are. Search the house, Breen. I'll cover the street door."

The man he called Breen went upstairs on the jump, and Mason continued. "Tell the story, one of you. Who is this man? Who killed him?"

As he talked, the inspector was examining Somers' body, making rapid notes in a little book, keeping his eye on the door, and darting quick glances at each of us, as he tried to grasp the situation.

I looked at Bert Garrison, who was perhaps the most favored of Miss Van Allen's friends, but he shook his head, so I threw myself into the breach.

"Inspector," I said, "that man's name is Somers. Further than that I know nothing. He is a stranger to all of us, and he came to this house to-night for the first time in his life."

"How'd he happen to come? Friend of Miss Van Allen?"

"He met her to-night for the first time. He came here with—" I paused. It was so hard to know what to do. Steele had gone home, ought I to implicate him?

"Go on—came here with whom? The truth, now."

"I usually speak the truth" I returned, shortly. "He came with Mr. Norman Steele."

"Where is Mr. Steele?"

"He has gone. There were a great many people here, and, naturally, some of them went away when this tragedy was discovered."

"Humph! Then, of course, the guilty party escaped. But we are getting nowhere. Does nobody know anything of this man, but his name?"

Nobody did; but Ariadne piped up, "He was a delightful man. He told me he was a great patron of art, and often bought pictures."

Paying little heed to her, the inspector was endeavoring to learn from the dead man's property something more about him.

"No letters or papers," he said, disappointedly, as he turned out the pockets. "Not unusual—in evening togs— but not even a card or anything personal—looks queer—"

"Look in his watch," said Ariadne, bridling with importance.

Giving her a keen glance, the inspector followed her suggestion. In the back of the case was a picture of a coquettish face, undoubtedly that of an actress. It was not carefully fastened in, but roughly cut out and pressed in with ragged edges.

"Temporary," grunted the inspector, "and recently stuck in. Some chicken he took out to supper. He's a club man, you say?"

"Yes, Mr. Steele said so, and also vouched for his worth and character." I resented the inspector's attitude. Though I knew nothing of Somers, and didn't altogether like him, yet, I saw no reason to think ill of the dead, until circumstances warranted it.

Further search brought a thick roll of money, some loose silver, a key-ring with seven or eight keys, eyeglasses in a silver case, handkerchiefs, a gold pencil, a knife, and such trifles as any man might have in his pockets, but no directly identifying piece of property.

R. S. was embroidered in tiny white letters on the handkerchiefs, and a monogram R. S. was on his seal ring.

His jewelry, which was costly, the inspector did not touch. There were magnificent pearl studs, a watch fob, set with a black opal and pearl cufflinks. Examination of his hat showed the pierced letters R. S., but nothing gave clue to his Christian name.

"Somers," said the inspector, musingly. "What club does he belong to?"

"I don't know," I replied. "Mr. Steele belongs to several, but Mr. Somers does not belong to any that I do. At least, I've never seen him at any."

"Call in the servants. Let's find out something about this household."

As no one else moved to do it, I stepped to the door of the butler's pantry, and summoned the head waiter of the caterer.

"Where are the house servants?" I asked him.

"There aren't any, sir," he replied, looking shudderingly at the grisly form on the floor.

"No servants? In a house of this type! What do you mean?"

"That's true," said Mrs. Reeves, breaking her silence, at last. "Miss Van Allen has a very capable woman, who is housekeeper and ladies' maid in one. But when guests are here, the suppers are served from the caterer's."

"Then call the housekeeper. And where is Miss Van Allen herself?"

"She's not in the house," said the policeman Breen, returning from his search.

"Not in the house!" cried Mrs. Reeves. "Where is she?"

"I've been all over—every room—every floor. She isn't in the house. There's nobody upstairs at all."

"No housekeeper or maid?" demanded Mason. "Then they've got away! Here, waiter, tell me all you know of this thing."

The Italian Luigi came forward, shaking with terror, and wringing his fingers nervously.

"I d—don't know anything about it," he began, but Mason interrupted, "You do! You know all about it! Did you kill this man?"

"No! Dio mio! No! a thousand no's!"

"Then, unless you wish to be suspected of it, tell all you know."

A commotion at the door heralded the coroner's arrival, also a detective and a couple of plain clothes men. Clearly, here was a mysterious case.

The coroner at once took matters in his own hands. Inspector Mason told him all that had been learned so far, and though Coroner Fenn seemed to think matters had been pretty well bungled, he made no comment and proceeded with the inquiries.

"Sure there's nobody upstairs?" he asked Breen.

"Positive. I looked in every nook and cranny. I've raked the whole house, but the basement and kitchen part."

"Go down there, then, and then go back and search upstairs again. Somebody may be hiding. Who here knows Miss Van Allen the most intimately?"

"Perhaps I do," said Mrs. Reeves. "Or Miss Gale. We are both her warm friends."

"I'm also her friend," volunteered Bert Garrison. "And I can guarantee that if Miss Van Allen has fled from this house it was out of sheer fright. She never saw this man until to-night. He was a stranger to us all."

"Where's the housekeeper?" went on Fenn.

"I think she must be somewhere about," said Mrs. Reeves. "Perhaps in the kitchen. Julie is an all round capable woman. When there are no guests she prepares Miss Van Allen's meals herself. When company is present the caterer always is employed."

"And there are no other servants?"

"Not permanent ones," replied Mrs. Reeves. "I believe the laundress and chore boy come by the day, also cleaning women and such. But I know that Miss Van Allen has no resident servant besides the maid Julie."

"This woman must be found," snapped the coroner. "But we must first of all identify the body. Mason, call up the principal clubs on the telephone, and locate R. Somers. Also find Mr. Norman Steele. Now, Luigi, let's have your story."

The trembling waiter stammered incoherently, and said little of moment.

"Look here," said Fenn, bluntly, "is that your knife sticking in him? I mean, is it one belonging to Fraschini's service? Don't touch it, but look at it, you can tell."

Luigi leaned over the dead man. "Yes, it is one of our boning knives," he said. "We always bring our own hardware."

"Well, then, if you want to clear yourself and your men of doubt, tell all you know."

"I know this," and Luigi braced himself to the ordeal. "I was waiting in the pantry for Miss Van Allen to send me word to serve supper, and I peeped in the dining-room now and then to see if it was time. I heard, presently, Miss Van Allen's voice, also a man's voice. I didn't want to intrude, so waited for a summons. After a moment or two I heard a little scream, and heard somebody or something fall. I had no thought of anything wrong, but thought the guests were unusually—er—riotous."

"Are Miss Van Allen's guests inclined to be riotous?"

"No, sir, oh, no," asseverated the man, while Mrs. Reeves and Ariadne looked indignant. "And for that reason, I felt a little curious, so I pushed the door ajar and peeped in."

"What did you see?"

"I saw," Luigi paused so long that I feared he was going to collapse. But the coroner eyed him sternly, and he went on. "I saw Miss Van Allen standing, looking down at this—this gentleman on the floor, and making as if to pull out the knife. I could scarcely believe my eyes, and I watched her. She didn't pull the knife, but she straightened up, looked around, glanced down at her gown, which—which was stained with blood—and then— she ran out into the hall."

"Where did she go?"

"I don't know. I couldn't see, as the door was but on a crack. Then I thought I ought to go into the dining-room, and I did. I looked at the gentleman, and I didn't know what to do. So I went into the hall, to the parlor door, and called for help, for a doctor or somebody. And then they all came out here. That's all I know."

Luigi's nerve gave way, and he sank into a chair with a sob. Fenn looked at him, and considerately left him alone for the time.

"Can this be true?" he said, turning to us. "Can you suspect Miss Van Allen of this crime?"

"No!" cried Bert Garrison and the women, at once. And, "No!" said I. "I am positive Miss Van Allen did not know Mr. Somers and could not have killed an utter stranger—on no provocation whatever."

"You do not know what provocation she may have had," suggested Fenn.

"Now, look here, Mr. Coroner," said Mrs. Reeves very decidedly, "I won't have Miss Van Allen spoken of in any such way. I assume you mean that this man, though a stranger, might have said or done something to annoy or offend Miss Van Allen. Well, if he had done so, Victoria Van Allen never would have killed him! She is the gentlest, most gay and light-hearted girl, and though she never tolerates any rudeness or familiarity, the idea of her killing a man is too absurd. You might as well suspect a dove or a butterfly of crime!"

"That's right, Mr. Coroner," said Garrison. "That waiter's story is an hallucination of some sort—if it isn't a deliberate falsification. Miss Van Allen is a dainty, happy creature, and to connect her with anything like this is absurd!"

"That's to be found out, Mr. Garrison. "Why did Miss Van Allen run away?"

"I don't admit that she did run away—in the sense of flight. If she were frightened at this thing—if she saw it— she may have run out of the door in hysterics or in a panic of terror. But she the perpetrator! Never!"

"Never!" echoed Mrs. Reeves. "The poor child! If she did come out here—and saw this awful sight—why, I think it would unhinge her mind!"

"Who is Miss Van Allen?" asked Fenn. "What is her occupation?"

"She hasn't an occupation," said Mrs. Reeves. "She is a young lady of independent fortune. As to her people or immediate relatives, I know nothing at all. I've known her a year or so, and as she never referred to such matters I never inquired. But she's a thorough little gentlewoman, and I'll defend her against any slander to my utmost powers."

"And so will I," said Miss Gale. "I'm sure of her fineness of character, and lovely nature—"

"But these opinions, ladies, don't help our inquiries," interrupted Fenn. "What can you men tell us? What I want first, is to identify this body, or, rather to learn more of R. Somers, and to find Miss Van Allen. I can't hold an inquest until these points are cleared up. Mason, have you found out anything?"

"No," said the inspector, returning from his long telephone quest. "I called up four clubs. Norman Steele belongs to three of them, but this man doesn't seem to belong to any. That is, there are Somerses and even R. Somerses, but they all have middle names, and, too, their description doesn't fit this Somers."

"Then Mr. Steele misrepresented him. Did you get Steele, Mason?"

"No, he wasn't at any of the clubs. I found his residence, a bachelor apartment house, but he isn't there, either."

"Find Steele; find Miss Van Allen; find the maid, what's her name—Julia?"

"Julie, she was always called," said Mrs. Reeves. "If Miss Van Allen went away, I've no doubt Julie went with her. She is a most devoted caretaker of her mistress."

"An oldish woman?"

"No. Perhaps between thirty-five and forty."

"What's she look like?"

"Describe her, Ariadne, you're an artist."

"Julie," said Miss Gale, "is a good sort. She's medium-sized, she has brown hair and rather hazel eyes. She wears glasses, and she stoops a little in her walk. She has perfect training and correct manners, and she is a model servant, but she gives the impression of watching over Miss Van Allen, whatever else she may be engaged in at the same time."

"Wears black?"

"No; usually gray gowns, or sometimes white. Inconspicuous aprons and no cap. She's not quite a menial, but yet, not entirely a housekeeper."

"English?"

"English speaking, if that's what you mean. But I think she's an American. Don't you, Mrs Reeves?"

"American? Yes, of course."

CHAPTER 4: SOMERS' REAL NAME

Detective Lowney, who had come with the coroner, had said little but had listened to all. Occasionally he would dart from the room, and return a few moments later, scribbling in his notebook. He was an alert little man, with beady black eyes and a stubby black mustache.

"I want a few words with that caterer's man," he said, suddenly, "and then they'd better clear away this supper business and go home."

We all turned to look at the table. It stood in the end of the dining-room that was back of the living-room. The sideboard was at the opposite end, back of the hall, and it was directly in front of the sideboard that Somers' body lay.

Lowney turned on more light, and a thrill went through us at the incongruity of that gay table and the tragedy so near it. As always at Vicky Van's parties, the appointments were dainty and elaborate. Flowers decorated the table; lace, silver, and glass were of finest quality; and in the centre was the contrivance known as a "Jack Horner Pie."

"That was to be the surprise," said Mrs. Reeves. "I knew about it. The pie is full of lovely trinkets and little jokes on the guests."

"I thought those things were for children's parties," observed Fenn, looking with interest at the gorgeous confection.

"They're really for birthdays," said Mrs. Reeves, "and to-day is Vicky's birthday. That was part of her surprise. She didn't want it known, lest the guests should bring gifts. She's like a child, Vicky is, just as happy over a birthday party as a little girl would be."

"What does Miss Van Allen look like?" asked the detective.

"She's pretty," replied Mrs. Reeves, "awfully pretty, but not a raving beauty. Black hair, and bright, fresh coloring—"

"How was she dressed? Giddy clothes?"

"In an evening gown," returned Mrs. Reeves, who resented the detective's off-hand manner. "A beautiful French gown, of tulle and gold trimmings."

"Low-necked, and all that? Jewels?"

"Yes," I said, as Mrs. Reeves disdained to answer. "Full evening costume, and a necklace and earrings of amber set in gold."

"Well, what I'm getting at is," said Lowney, "a woman dressed like that couldn't go very far in the streets without being noticed. We'll surely be able to trace Miss Van Allen. Where would she be likely to go?"

"I don't know," said Mrs. Reeves. "She wouldn't go to my home, I live 'way down in Washington Square."

"Nor to mine," chirped Ariadne, "it's over on the west side."

"I don't believe she left the house," declared the coroner.

"Tell us again, Luigi," asked Lowney, "just where did the lady seem to go, when you saw her leave this room?"

"I can't say, sir. I was looking through a small opening, as I pushed the door ajar, and I was so amazed at what I saw, that I was sort of paralyzed and didn't dare open the door further."

"Go back to the pantry," commanded Fenn, "and look in, just as you did."

The waiter retreated to the post he had held, and setting the door a few inches ajar, proved that he could see body by the sideboard, but could not command a view of the hall.

"Now, I'll represent Miss Van Allen," and Lowney stood over the body of Somers. "Is this the place?"

"A little farther to the right, sir," and Luigi's earnestness and good faith were unmistakable. "Yes, sir, just there."

"Now, I walk out into the hall. Is this the way she went?"

"Yes, sir, the same."

Lowney went from the dining-room to the hall, and it was clear that his further progress could not be seen by the peeping waiter.

"You see, Fenn," the detective went on, "from here, in the back of this long hall, Miss Van Allen could have left the house by two ways. She could have gone out at the front door, passing the parlor, or, she could have gone down these basement stairs, which are just under the stairs to the second story. Then she could have gone out by the front area door, which would give her access to the street. She could have caught up a cloak as she went."

"Or," said Fenn, musingly, "she could have run upstairs. The staircase is so far back in the hall, that the guests in the parlor would not have seen her. This is a very deep house, you see."

It was true. The stairs began so far back in the long hall, that Vicky could easily have slipped upstairs after leaving the dining-room, without being seen by any of us in the living-room, unless we were in its doorway, looking out. Was anybody? So many guests had left, that this point could not be revealed.

"I didn't see her," declared Mrs. Reeves, "and I don't believe she was in the dining-room at all. I don't care what that waiter says!"

"Oh, yes, Madame," reiterated Luigi. "It was Miss Van Allen. I know her well. Often she comes to Fraschini's, and always I take her orders. She came even this afternoon, to make sure the great cake—the Jack Horner, was all right. And she approved it, ah, she clapped her hands at sight of it. We all do our best for Miss Van Allen, she is a lovely lady."

"Miss Van Allen is one of your regular customers?"

"One of our best. Very often we serve her, and always she orders our finest wares."

"You provide everything?"

"Everything. Candles, flowers, decorations—all"

"And she pays her bills?"

"Most promptly."

"By cheque?"

"Yes, sir."

"And there are no servants here but the maid Julie?"

"I have often seen others. But I fancy they do not live in the house. Madame Julie superintends and directs us always. Miss Van Allen leaves much to her. She is most capable."

"When did you see this woman, this Julie, last?"

"A short time before—before that happened." Luigi looked toward the body. "She was in and out of the pantries all the evening. She admitted the guests, she acted as ladies' maid, and she arranged the favors in the pie. It was, I should say, ten minutes or so since she was last in the pantry, when I peeped in at the door."

"Where was Julie then?"

"I don't know. I did not see her. Perhaps upstairs, or maybe in the front of the hall, waiting to bring me word to serve supper."

"Tell me something distinctive about this maid's appearance. Was she good-looking?"

"Yes, a good-looking woman. But nothing especial about her. She had many gold fillings in her teeth—"

"That's something," and Lowney noted it with satisfaction. "Go on."

But Luigi seemed to know nothing else that differentiated Julie from her sisters in service, and Lowney changed his questions.

"How could Miss Van Allen get that knife of yours?" he asked.

"I don't know, sir. It was, I suppose, in the pantry, with our other knives."

"What is its use?"

"It is a boning knife, but doubtless one of our men used it in cutting celery for salad, or some such purpose."

"Ask them."

Inquiry showed that a man, named Palma, had used the knife for making a salad, and had left it in the butler's pantry an hour or so before the crime was committed. Any one could have taken the knife without its being missed, as the salad had been completed and put aside.

"In that case, Miss Van Allen must have secured the knife some little time before it was used, as Luigi was in the pantry just previously," observed Fenn. "That shows premeditation. It wasn't done with a weapon picked up at the moment."

"Then it couldn't have been done by Miss Van Allen!" exclaimed Mrs. Reeves triumphantly, "for Vicky had no reason to premeditate killing a man she had never seen before."

"Vicky didn't do it," wailed Ariadne. "I know she didn't."

"She must be found," said Lowney. "But she will be found. If she's innocent, she will return herself. If guilty, we must find her. And we will. A householder cannot drop out of existence unnoticed by any one. Does she own this house?"

"I think so," said Mrs. Reeves. "I'm not positive, but it's my impression that she does. Vicky Van never boasts or talks of her money or of herself. But I know she gives a good deal in charity, and is always ready to subscribe to philanthropic causes. I tell you she is not the criminal, and I don't believe she ever left this house in the middle of the night in evening dress! That child is scared to death, and is hiding—in the attic or somewhere."

"Suppose, Mrs. Reeves," said the coroner, "you go with Mr. Lowney, and look over the house again. Search the bedrooms and store-rooms."

"I will," and Mrs. Reeves seemed to welcome an opportunity to help. She was a good-hearted woman, and a staunch friend of Vicky Van. I was glad she was on hand to stand up for the girl, for I confess things looked, to me, pretty dubious.

"Come along, too, Mr. Calhoun," said Mrs. Reeves. "There's no telling what we may find. Perhaps there's further—tragedy."

I knew what was in her mind. That if Vicky had done the thing, she might have, in an agony of remorse, taken her own life.

Thrilled with this new fear, I followed Lowney and Mrs. Reeves. We went downstairs first. We examined all the basement rooms and the small, city back yard. There was no sign of Vicky Van or of Julie, and next we came back to the first floor, hunted that, and then on upstairs. The music room was soon searched, and I fell back as the others went into Vicky's bedroom.

"Come on, Mr. Calhoun," said Lowney, "we must make a thorough job of it this time."

The bedroom was, it seemed to me, like a fairy dream. Furniture of white enameled wicker, with pink satin cushions. Everywhere the most exquisite appointments of silver, crystal and embroidered fabrics, and a bed fit for a princess. It seemed profanation for the little detective to poke and pry around in wardrobes and cupboards, though I knew it must be done. He was not only looking for Vicky, but noting anything that might bear on her disappearance.

But there was no clue. Everything was in order, and all just as a well-bred, refined woman would have her belongings.

The bedroom was over the dining-room, and back of this, over the pantry extension, was Vicky Van's dressing-room.

This was a bijou boudoir, and dressing-table, chiffonier, robe-chests, and jewel-caskets were all in keeping with the personality of their owner. The walls were panelled in pale rose color, and a few fine pictures were in absolute harmony. A long mirror was in a Florentine gilt frame, and a chaise longue, by a reading table, bespoke hours of ease.

Ruthlessly, Lowney pried into everything, ran his arm among the gowns hanging in the wardrobe, and looked into the carved chests.

Again no clue. The perfect order everywhere, showed, perhaps, preparation for guests, but nothing indicated flight or hiding. The dressing-table boxes held some bits of jewelry but nothing of really great value. An escritoire was full of letters and papers, and this, Lowney locked, and put the key in his pocket.

"If it's all right," he said, "there's no harm done. And if the lady doesn't show up, we must examine the stuff."

On we went to the third floor of the house. The rooms here were unused, save one that was evidently Julie's. The furnishings, though simple, were attractive, and showed a thoughtful mistress and an appreciative maid. Everything was in order. Several uniforms of black and of gray were in the cupboard, and several white aprons and one white dress. There were books, and a work-basket and such things as betokened the life of a sedate, busy woman.

We left no room, no cupboard unopened. No hall or loft unsearched. We looked in, under and behind every piece of furniture, and came, at last, to the unescapable conclusion that wherever Vicky Van might be, she was not in her own house.

Downstairs we went, and found Coroner Fenn and Inspector Mason in the hall. They had let Doctor Remson go home, also Garrison and Miss Gale. The waiters, too, had been sent off.

"You people can go, if you like," Fenn said, to Mrs. Reeves and myself. "I'll take your addresses, and you can expect to be called on as witnesses. If we ever get anything to witness! I never saw such a case! No criminal to arrest, and nobody knows the victim! He must be from out of town. We'll nail Mr. Steele to-morrow, and begin to get somewhere. Also we'll look up Miss Van Allen's credits and business acquaintances. A woman can't have lived two years in a house like this, and not have somebody know her antecedents and relatives. I suppose Mr. Steele brought his friend here, and then, when this thing happened he was scared and lit out."

"Maybe Steele did the killing," suggested Lowney.

"No," disagreed Fenn. "I believe that Dago waiter's yarn. I cross-questioned him a lot before I let him go, and I'm sure he's telling what he saw. I'll see Fraschini's head man to-morrow—or, I suppose it's to-morrow now—hello, who's that?"

Another policeman came in at the street door.

"What's up?" he said, looking about in amazement. "You here, Mr. Fenn? Lowney? What's doing?"

It was Patrolman Ferrall, the officer on the beat.

"Where you been?" asked the coroner. "Don't you know what has happened?"

"No; ever since midnight I been handling a crowd at a fire a couple blocks away. This is Miss Van Allen's house."

"Sure it is, and a friend of hers named Somers has been bumped off."

"What? Killed?"

"That's it. What do you know of Miss Van Allen?"

"Nothing, except that she lives here. Quiet young lady. Nothin' to be said about her. Who's the man?"

"Don't know, except named Somers. R. Somers."

"Never heard of him. Where's Miss Van Allen?"

"Skipped."

"What! That little thoroughbred can't be mixed up in a shootin'!"

"He isn't shot. Stabbed. With a kitchen knife."

"Let's see him."

The coroner and Ferrall went toward the dining room, and, on an irresistible impulse of curiosity, I followed.

"Him!" exclaimed Ferrall, as he caught sight of the dead man's features. "That ain't no Somers. That's Randolph Schuyler."

"What!"

"Sure it is. Schuyler, the millionaire. Lives on Fifth Avenue, not far down from here. Who killed him?"

"But look here. Are you sure this is Randolph Schuyler?"

"Sure? Of course I'm sure. His house is on my beat. I see him often, goin' in or comin' out."

"Well, then we have got a big case on our hands! Mason!"

The inspector could scarcely believe Ferrall's statement, but realized that the policeman must know.

"Whew!" he said, trying to think of a dozen things at once. "Then Steele knew him, and introduced him as Somers on purpose. No wonder the clubs didn't know of R. Somers! R. S. on his handkerchiefs and all that. He used a false name 'cause he didn't want it known that Randolph Schuyler came to see Miss Van Allen! Oh, here's a mess! Where's that girl? Why did she kill him?"

"She didn't!" Mrs. Reeves began to cry. "She didn't know it was Mr. Schuyler. She doesn't know Mr. Schuyler. I'm sure she doesn't, because we were making lists for bazar patrons and she said she would ask only people she knew, and we tried to find somebody who knew Randolph Schuyler, to ask him, but we didn't know anybody who was acquainted with him at all. Oh, it can't be the rich Schuyler! Why would he come here?"

"We must get hold of Mr. Steele as soon as possible," said Fenn, excitedly. "Breen, call up his home address again, and if he isn't there, go there and stick till he comes. Now, for some one to identify this body. Call up the Schuyler house—no, better go around there. Where is it, Ferrall?"

"Go straight out to the Avenue, and turn down. It's No.—only part of a block down. Who's going?"

"You go, Lowney," said Fenn. "Mason, will you go?"

"Yes, of course. Come on, Lowney."

The coroner gave Mrs. Reeves and myself permission to go home, and I was glad to go. But Mrs. Reeves declared her intention of staying the night, what was left of it, in Miss Van Allen's house.

"It's too late for me to go down alone," she said, in her sensible way. "And, too, I'd rather be here, in case—in case Miss Van Allen comes home. I'm her friend, and I know she'd like me to stay."

CHAPTER 5: THE SCHUYLER HOUSEHOLD

As for me, I began to collect my senses after the shock of learning the true identity of the dead man. Though I had never met him, Randolph Schuyler was a client and friend of my partner, Charles Bradbury, and I suddenly felt a sort of personal responsibility of action.

For one thing, I disliked the idea of Mr. Schuyler's wife and family receiving the first tidings of the tragedy from the police. It seemed to me a friend ought to break the news, if possible.

I said as much to Coroner Fenn, and he agreed.

"That's so," he said. "It'll be an awful errand. In the middle of the night, too. If you're acquainted, suppose you go there with the boys, Mr. Calhoun."

"I'm not personally acquainted, but Mr. Schuyler is my partner's client, though there's been little business of his with our firm of late. But, as a matter of humanity, I'll go, if you say so, and be of any help I can."

"Go, by all means. Probably they'll be glad of your advice and assistance in many ways."

I dreaded the errand, yet I thought if the police had had to go and tell Winnie and Aunt Lucy any such awful news, how glad they'd be to have somebody present of their own world, even of their own neighborhood. So I went.

As we had been told, the Schuyler house was only a few doors below the Avenue corner. Even as Mason rang the bell, I was thinking how strange that a man should go to a house where he desired to conceal his own name, when it was so near his own dwelling.

And yet, I knew, too, that the houses on Fifth Avenue are as far removed from houses just off the Avenue, as if they were in a different town.

Mason's ring was answered by a keen-eyed man of imperturbable countenance.

"What's wanted?" he said, gazing calmly at the policemen.

"Where is Mr. Schuyler?" asked the inspector, in a matter-of-fact way.

"He's out," said the man, respectfully enough, but of no mind to be loquacious.

"Where?"

"I don't know. He went to his club after dinner, and has not yet returned."

"Are you his valet?"

"Yes, I wait up for him. He comes in with his key. I've no idea when he will return."

"Is his wife at home?"

"Yes, Mrs. Schuyler is at home." Clearly, this man was answering questions only because he recognized the authority that asked them. But he volunteered no information.

"Who else is in the family? Children?"

"No, Mr. Schuyler has no children. His two sisters are here, and Mrs. Schuyler. That is all."

"They are all in bed?"

"Yes, sir. Has anything happened to Mr. Schuyler?"

"Yes, there has. Mr. Schuyler is dead."

"Dead!" The imperturbable calm gave way, and the valet became nervously excited. "What do you mean? Where is he? Shall I go to him?"

"We will come in," said Lowney, for until now, we had stood outside. "Then we will tell you. Are any of the other servants about?"

"No, sir, they are all in bed."

"Then—what is your name?"

"Cooper, sir."

"Then, Cooper, call the butler, or whoever is in general charge. And—summon Mrs. Schuyler."

"I'll call Jepson, he's the butler, sir. And I'll call Mrs. Schuyler's maid, Tibbetts, if she's in. And the maid, Hester, who waits on the Misses Schuyler. Shall I?"

"Yes, get things started. Get Jepson as soon as you can."

"This is an awful affair," said Mason, as Cooper went off. We were in the hall, a great apartment more like a room, save that a broad staircase curved up at one side. The furnishings were magnificent, but in a taste heavily ornate and a little old-fashioned. There were carved and upholstered benches, but none of us cared to sit. The tension was too great.

"Keep your eyes open, Lowney," he went on. "There's lots to be picked up from servants, before they're really on their guard. Get all you can about Mr. Schuyler's evening habits from the man, Cooper. But go easy with the ladies. It's hard enough for them at best."

The valet reappeared with Jepson. This butler was of the accepted type, portly and important, but the staggering news Cooper had evidently told him, had made him a man among men.

"What's this?" he said, gravely. "The master dead? Apoplexy?"

"No, Jepson. Mr. Schuyler was killed by some one. We don't know who did it."

"Killed! Murdered! My God!" The butler spoke in a strong, low voice with no hint of dramatic effect. "How will Mrs. Schuyler bear it?"

"How shall we tell her, Jepson?" Mason showed a consultant air, for the butler was so evidently a man of judgment and sense.

"We must waken her maid, and let her rouse Mrs. Schuyler. Then the other ladies, Mr. Schuyler's sisters, we must call them."

"Yes, Jepson, do all those things, as quickly as you can."

But the wait seemed interminable.

At last the butler came back, and asked us up to the library, the front room on the floor above. Here a footman was lighting a fire on the hearth, for the house had the chill of the small hours.

First came the two sisters. These ladies, though not elderly, were middle-aged, and perhaps, a few years older than their brother. They were austere and prim, of aristocratic features and patrician air.

But they were almost hysterical in their excitement. A distressed maid hovered behind them with sal volatile. The ladies were fully attired, but caps on their heads and woolly wraps flung round them bore witness to hasty dressing.

"What is it?" cried Miss Rhoda, the younger of the two. "What has happened to Randolph?"

I introduced myself to them. I told them, as gently as I could, the bare facts, deeming it wise to make no prevarication.

So raptly did they listen and so earnestly did I try to omit horrible details, and yet tell the truth, that I did not hear Mrs. Schuyler enter the room. But she did come in, and heard also, the story as I told it.

"Can it not be," I heard a soft voice behind me say, "can it not yet be there is some mistake? Who says that man is my husband?"

I turned to see the white face and clenched hands of Randolph Schuyler's widow. She was holding herself together, and trying to get a gleam of hope from uncertainty.

If I had felt pity and sorrow for her before I saw her, it was doubly poignant now.

Ruth Schuyler was one of those gentle, appealing women, helplessly feminine in emergency. Her frightened, grief-stricken eyes looked out of a small, pale face, and her bloodless lips quivered as she caught them between her teeth in an effort to preserve her self-control.

"I am Chester Calhoun," I said, and she bowed in acknowledgment. "I am junior partner in the firm of

Bradbury and Calhoun. Mr. Bradbury is one of your husband's lawyers and also a friend, so, as circumstances brought it about, I came here, with Inspector Mason, to tell you—to tell you—"

Mrs. Schuyler sank into a seat. Still with that air of determination to be calm, she gripped the chair arms and said, "I heard you tell Miss Schuyler that Randolph has been killed. I ask you, may it not be some one else? Why should he be at a house where people called him by a name not his own?"

She had heard, then, all I had told the older ladies. For Mrs. Schuyler was not old. She must be, I thought at once, years younger than her husband. Perhaps a second wife. I was glad she had heard, for it saved repeating the awful narrative.

"He has not been identified, Mrs. Schuyler," I said, "except by the policeman of this precinct, who declares he knows him well."

I was glad to give her this tiny loophole of possibility of mistaken identity, and she eagerly grasped at it.

"You must make sure," she said, looking at Inspector Mason.

"I'm afraid there's no room for doubt, ma'am, but I'm about to send the man, the valet, over to see him. Do you wish any one else to go—from the house?"

Mrs. Schuyler shuddered. "Don't ask me to go," she said, piteously. "For I can't think it is really Mr. Schuyler—and if it should be—"

"Oh, no ma'am, you needn't go. None of the family, I should say." Mason looked at the elder ladies.

"No, no," cried Miss Sarah, "we couldn't think of it! But let Jepson go. He is a most reliable man."

"Yes," said Mrs. Schuyler, "send Cooper and Jepson both. Oh, go quickly—I cannot bear this suspense!" She turned to me, as the two men who had been hovering in the doorway, came in to take Mason's orders. "I thank you, Mr. Calhoun. It was truly kind of you to come. Tibbetts, get me a wrap, please."

This was Mrs. Schuyler's own maid, who went on the errand at once. More servants had gathered; one or two footmen, a silly French parlor-maid or waitress, and from downstairs I heard the hushed voices of others.

Tibbetts returned, and laid a fleecy white shawl about her mistress' shoulders. Mrs. Schuyler wore a house dress of dull blue. Her hair of an ash-blonde hue, was coiled on top of her head; and to my surprise, when I noticed it, she wore a string of large pearls round her throat, and on her hands were two rings, each set with an enormous pearl.

I must have been awkward enough to glance at the pearls, for Mrs. Schuyler remarked, "I dressed so hastily, I kept on my pearls. I wear them at night sometimes, to preserve their luster."

Then she apparently forgot them, for without self-consciousness she turned to the detective and began asking questions. Nervously she inquired concerning minutest details, and I surmised that side by side with her grief at the tragedy was a very human and feminine dismay at the thought of her husband, stabbed to death in another woman's house!

"Who is Miss Van Allen?" she asked over and over again, unsatisfied with the scant information Lowney could give.

"And she lives near here? Just down the side street? Who is she?"

"I don't think she is anyone you ever heard of," I said to her. "She is a pleasant young woman, and so far as I know, all that is correct and proper."

"Then why would she have Randolph Schuyler visiting her?" flashed the retort. "Is that correct and proper?"

"It may be so," I said, for I felt a sort of loyalty to Vicky Van. "You see, she was not acquainted with Mr. Schuyler until this evening."

"Why did he go there, then?"

"Steele brought him—Norman Steele."

"I don't know any Mr. Steele."

I began to think that Randolph Schuyler had possessed many acquaintances of whom his wife knew nothing, and I concluded to see Bradbury before I revealed any more of Schuyler's affairs.

And then, Lowney began adroitly to put questions instead of answering them.

He inquired concerning Mr. Schuyler's habits and pursuits, his recreations and his social life.

All three of the women gave responses to these queries, and I learned many things.

First, that Randolph Schuyler was one manner of man at home and another abroad. The household, it was plain to be seen, was one of most conservative customs and rigidly straightbacked in its conventions.

Mrs. Schuyler was not a second wife. She had been married about seven years, and had lived the last five of them in the house we were now in. She was much younger than her husband, and he had, I could see, kept her from all knowledge of or participation in his Bohemian tastes. They were the sort of people who have a box at the opera and are patrons of the best and most exclusive functions of the highest society. Mrs. Schuyler, after the first shock, recovered her poise, and though now and then a tremor shook her slight frame, she bore herself with dignity and calm.

The two maiden ladies also grew quieter, but we all nervously awaited the return of the butler.

At last he came.

"It's the master, Madame," he said, simply, to his mistress as he entered the room. "He is dead."

The deferential gravity of his tone impressed me anew with the man's worth, and I felt that the stricken wife had a tower of strength in the faithful servitor.

"I left Cooper there, Madame," he went on. "They— they will not bring Mr. Schuyler home tonight. In the morning, perhaps. And now, Madame, will you not go to rest? I will be at the service of these gentlemen."

It seemed cruel to torture them further that night, and the three ladies were dismissed by Lowney, and, attended by their maids, they left us.

"Now, Jepson," Lowney began, "tell us all you know about Mr. Schuyler's doings. I daresay you know as much as the valet does. Was Mr. Schuyler as a man of the world, different from his life in this house?"

Jepson looked perturbed. "That's not for me to say, sir."

"Oh, yes, it is, my man. The law asks you, and it is for you to tell all you know."

"Well, then," and the butler weighed his words, "my master was always most strict of habit in his home. The ladies are very reserved, and abide by rules and standards, that are, if I may say so, out of date to-day. But, though Mr. Schuyler was by no means a gay man or a member of any fast set, yet I have reason to think, sir, that at times he might go to places where he would not take Mrs. Schuyler, and where he would not wish Mrs. Schuyler to know he had been himself."

"That's enough," said Lowney. "I've got his number. Now, Jepson, had your master any enemies, that you know of?"

"Not that I know of. But I know nothing of Mr. Schuyler's affairs. I see him go out of an evening, and I may notice that he comes in very late, but as to his friends or enemies, I know nothing at all. I am not one to pry, sir, and my master has always trusted me. I have endeavored not to betray that trust."

This might have sounded pharisaical in a man of less sincerity of speech. But Jepson's clear, straightforward eyes forbade any doubt of his honesty and truth.

Again I was glad that Mrs. Schuyler had this staunch helper at her side, for I foresaw troublous times in store for her.

"And you never heard of this Miss Van Allen? Never was in her house before?"

"Never, sir. I know nothing of the houses on the side blocks." I winced at this. "Of course, I know the people who come to this house, but there is among them no Miss Van Allen."

"Rather not!" I thought to myself. And then I sighed at the memory of Vicky Van. Had she killed this millionaire? And if so, why?

I was sure Vicky had never met Randolph Schuyler before that evening. I had seen their meeting, and it was too surely the glance of stranger to stranger that had passed between them, to make a previous acquaintance possible. Vicky had been charming to him, as she always was to every one, but she showed no special interest, and if she did really kill him, it was some unguessable motive that prompted the deed.

I thought it over. Schuyler, at the club, dined and wined, had perhaps heard Norman Steele extol the charms of Vicky Van. Interested, he had asked to be taken to Vicky's house, but, as it was so near his own, a sense of precaution led him to adopt another name.

Then the inexplicable sequel!

And the mysterious disappearance of Vicky herself.

Though, of course, the girl would return. As Mrs. Reeves had said, doubtless she had witnessed the crime, and, scared out of her wits, had run away. Her return would clear up the matter.

Then the waiter's story?

Well, there was much to be done. And, as I suddenly bethought me, it was time I, myself went home!

As I passed Vicky Van's house, on my way home, I saw lights pretty much all over it, and was strongly tempted to go in. But common sense told me I needed rest, and not only did I have many matters to attend to on the morrow, but I had to tell the story to Aunt Lucy and Winnie!

That, of itself, would require some thought and tactful management, for I was not willing to have them condemn Vicky Van entirely, and yet, I could think of no argument to put forth for the girl's innocence.

Time alone must tell.

CHAPTER 6: VICKY'S WAYS

"Ches-ter Cal-houn! Get up this minute! There's a reporter downstairs! A reporter!"

My sleepy eyes opened to find Winnie pounding my shoulder as it humped beneath the blanket.

"Hey? What?" I grunted, trying to collect my perceptions.

"A reporter!" If Winnie had said a Bengal tiger, she couldn't have looked more terrified.

"Great Scott! Win—I remember! Clear out, I'll be down in a minute."

I dressed in record time and went downstairs in three leaps.

In the library, I found Aunt Lucy, wearing an expression that she might have shown if the garbage man had asked her to a dance.

But Winnie was eagerly drinking in the story poured forth by the said reporter, who was quite evidently enjoying his audience.

"Oh, Chet, this is Mr. Bemis of The Meteor. He's telling us all about the—you know—what happened."

Winnie was too timid to say the word murder, and I was sorry she had to hear the awful tale from any one but myself. However, there was no help for it now, and I joined the group and did all I could to bring Aunt Lucy's eyebrows and nose down to their accustomed levels.

But it was an awful story, make the best of it, and the truth had to be told.

"It is appalling," conceded Aunt Lucy, at length, "but the most regrettable circumstance, to my mind, is your connection with it all, Chester."

"Now, Auntie, have a little heart for poor Mrs. Schuyler, and those old lady sisters. Also for the man himself—"

"Oh, I have, Chet. I'm not inhuman. But those things are in the papers every day, and while one feels a general sympathy, it can't be personal if one doesn't know the people. But, for you to be mixed up in such matters—"

"I wasn't mixed up in it, Aunt Lucy, except as I chose to mix myself. And I've no doubt I should have gotten into it anyway. Mr. Bradbury will have a lot to do with it, I'm sure. I'm no better than he to mix in."

"In a business way, yes. But you were there socially— where a murder was committed—"

Aunt Lucy could have shown no more horror of it all, if I had been the convicted criminal.

"And, I'm glad I was!" I cried, losing patience a little. "If I can be of any help to the Schuyler people or to Miss Van Allen, I shall be willing to do all I can.

"But Miss Van Allen is the—the murderer!" and Aunt Lucy whispered the word.

"Don't say that!" I cried sharply. "You don't know it at all, and there's no reason to condemn the girl—"

I paused. Bemis was taking in my every word with a canny understanding of what I said, and also of what I didn't say.

"Where do your suspicions tend, Mr. Calhoun?" he said smoothly.

"Frankly, Mr. Bemis, I don't know. I am an acquaintance of Miss Van Allen and I cannot reconcile the idea of crime with her happy, gentle nature. Nor can I see any reason to suspect the waiter who first told of the matter. But might not some person, some enemy of Mr. Schuyler, have been secreted in the house—"

"A plausible theory," agreed Bemis, "even an obvious one, but almost no chance of it. I've seen the caterer's people, and they were in charge of the basement rooms and the dining-room all the evening. Unless it were one of the guests at the party, I think no intruder could have gotten in."

"Well," I returned, uneasily, for I wished he would go, "it isn't up to us to invent theories or to defend them. I will answer your necessary questions, but pardon me, if I remind you that I am a busy man and I haven't yet had my breakfast."

Bemis took the hint, and after a string of definite and pertinent questions, he left.

Winnie tried to detain him, but my curt courtesy made it difficult for him to linger.

"Oh, Chessy," cried my sister, as soon as Bemis had gone, "it's awful, I know, but isn't it exciting?"

"Hush, Winnie," reproved Aunt Lucy. "A girl of your age should know nothing of these things, and I want you to put it out of your mind. You can be of no help, and I do not want your nerves disturbed by the harrowing details."

"That's all right, Aunt Lucy," I put in, "but this is going to be a celebrated case, and Winnie can't be kept in ignorance of its developments. Now be a good sort, Auntie—accept the inevitable. Try to realize that I must do what seems to me my duty, and if that brings us more or less into the limelight of publicity, it is a pity, but it can't be helped."

"I agree to all that, Chester, dear. But you are so mixed in it socially. Why did you ever get into that set?"

"It isn't a bad set, Aunt Lu. It isn't a fast set, by any means."

"You wouldn't see Winnie or me there."

"No, but a decent man goes to places where he wouldn't take his women people. Now, let up, Auntie. Trust your good-for-nothing nevvy, and just do all you can to help—by doing nothing."

"I'll help you, Chessy-Cat. I'll do exactly as you tell me, if you'll only let me know about it, and not treat me like a baby," said Winnie, who was wheedlesomely assisting my breakfast arrangements. She sugared and creamed my cereal, and, as I dispatched it, she buttered toast and poured coffee and deftly sliced off the top of a soft-boiled egg.

I managed to eat some of these viands between answers to their rapid-fire volley of questions and at last I made ready to go down town.

"And remember," I said, as I departed, "if a lot of gossippy old hens come around here to-day—or your chicken friends—Winnie, don't tell them a thing. Let 'em get it from the papers, or apply to information, or any old way, but don't you two give out a line of talk! See?"

I kissed them both, and started off.

Of course, I went over to Vicky Van's first. I had been on the proverbial pins and needles to get there ever since I woke to consciousness by reason of the sisterly pounding that brought me from the land of dreams.

The house had an inhabited look, and when I went in, I was greeted by the odor of boiling coffee.

"Come right down here," called Mrs. Reeves from the basement.

I went down, passing the closed dining-room door with a shudder. Two or three policemen were about, in charge of things generally, but none whom I knew. They had been relieved for the present.

"You're still here?" I said, a little inanely.

"Yes," returned Mrs. Reeves, who looked tired and wan. "I stayed, you know, but I couldn't sleep any. I lay down on the music-room couch, but I only dozed a few minutes at a time. I kept hearing strange sounds or imagining I did, and the police were back and forth till nearly daylight. Downstairs, they were. I didn't bother them, but they knew I was in the house, if—if Vicky should come home."

Her face was wistful and her eyes very sad. I looked my sympathy.

"You liked her, I know," she went on. "But everybody 'most, has turned against her. Since they found the man was Randolph Schuyler, all sympathy is for him and his widow. They all condemn Vicky."

"You can scarcely blame them," I began, but she interrupted,

"I do blame them! They've no right to accuse that girl unheard."

"The waiter—"

"Oh, yes, I know, the waiter! Well, don't let's quarrel about it. I can't stay here much longer, though. I made coffee and got myself some breakfast—but, honest, Mr. Calhoun, it pretty nearly choked me to eat sandwiches that had been made for last night's surprise supper!"

"I should think it would! Didn't any rolls come, or milk, you know?"

"I didn't see any. Well, I'll go home this morning, but I shall telephone up here every little while. The police will stay here, I suppose."

"Yes, for a day or two. Do you think Vicky will come back?"

"I don't know. She'll have to, sooner or later. I tried to make myself sleep in her room last night, but I just couldn't. So I stayed in the music room, I thought—I suppose it was foolish—but I thought maybe she might telephone."

"She'd hardly do that."

"I don't know. It's impossible to say what she might do. Oh, the whole thing is impossible! Think of it, Mr. Calhoun. Where could that girl have gone? Alone, at midnight, in that gorgeous gown, no hat or wrap—"

"How do you know that?"

"I don't—not positively. But if she had put on wraps and gone out by either door she would surely have been seen by some one in the house. I'm just sure she didn't go out by the front street door, for we in the living-room must have noticed her. And she couldn't have gone out by the area door, for there were waiters all about, down here."

We were sitting in the front basement room, a pleasant enough place, evidently a servants' sitting room. Before Mrs. Reeves, on the table, were the remnants of her scarce tasted breakfast. As she had said, the tiny sandwiches and rich salad, which she had procured from the unused stores of the caterer's provision, did seem too closely connected with the tragedy to be appetizing.

"The kitchen is back of this?" I asked.

"Yes, and dumb waiters to the dining-room. I confess I've looked about a bit. I'm not a prying woman—but I felt I was justified."

"You certainly are, Mrs. Reeves," I said, warmly, for she was thoroughly good-hearted, and a staunch friend of Vicky Van. "Have you learned anything illuminating?"

"No; but things are queer."

"Queer, how?"

"Well, you wouldn't understand. A man couldn't. But it's this way. Lots of potted meats and jars of jam and cans of tea and coffee and cocoa in the pantry, but no fresh meat or green vegetables about. No butter in the icebox, and no eggs or bacon."

"Well, what does that imply? I'm no housekeeper, I admit."

"It looks to me as if Vicky was leaving this morning—I mean as if she had expected to go away to-day, and so had no stuff on hand to spoil."

"Perhaps this is her market day."

"No; it's queer, that's what it is. You know sometimes Vicky does go away for days at a time."

"Hasn't she a right to?"

"Of course she has. I'm thinking it out. Where does she go? And wherever it is, that's where she is now!"

Mrs. Reeves' triumphant air seemed to settle the question.

"But all that isn't queer, my dear lady," I said. "We all know Vicky Van gads about a lot. I've telephoned her myself twice, and she wasn't here. Once, Julie answered, and once there was no response of any sort."

"Yes, I suppose that's the case. She was going away on a visit to-day, maybe, and so had little food on hand to be disposed of. A good housekeeper would look after that. Of course, it wouldn't be Vicky's doing, but Julie's. That housekeeper is a treasure. She could run a hotel if she wanted to."

"Then, perhaps," I mused, aloud, "Vicky ran away and went to the place, wherever it is, that she expected to visit to-day."

"Oh, I don't know. This is all merely conjecture. And, too, how could she, in that dress? No, she has gone to some friend in town. She must have done so. A hotel wouldn't take her in—why," Mrs. Reeves' voice broke, "you know that waiter said there—there was blood on Vicky's gown!"

"Do you believe that?"

"If we believe him at all, why shouldn't we believe the whole tale? I don't know Vicky Van, you understand, except as a casual friend. I mean, I know nothing of her family, her past, or her personality, except as I've seen her in a friendly way. I like her, thoroughly, but I can't honestly say that I know her."

"Who does?"

"Nobody. All her friends say the same thing. She is lovely and dear, but never confidential, or communicative regarding herself."

"Wherever she went, Julie must be with her," I suggested.

"I don't know. I dare say that is so, but how on earth could two women get out of this house without its being known?"

"And yet, they did. Whether alone or together, they both got away last night. You don't think they're still concealed in the house?"

"Oh, no, of course not; after the search we made."

"I can't help thinking they'll turn up to-day. Julie, anyway. Why, Miss Van Allen must come back or send back for her valuables. I saw jewelry and money in the dressing-room."

"Yes; but, of course, they're safe enough. They're all in care of the police."

We were interrupted by the entrance of a policeman and a woman who had come to work.

"She says," the policeman addressed Mrs. Reeves, "that she was expected here to-day to clean. Now, we can't let her disturb things much, but she'd better wash up a little, and throw away some of the supper stuff that won't keep."

Everybody seemed to look to Mrs. Reeves as a sort of proxy housekeeper, and I wondered what they would have done without her. Though I suppose they would have managed.

"Yes, indeed," was her glad response. "Let her tidy up these breakfast things I've used, and there's some cups and plates in the kitchen, for I gave those poor policemen some food 'long 'bout three o'clock this morning. And she can throw out the melted ice cream, it's no good to anybody, and it surely isn't evidence!"

I determined to ask the working-woman some questions, but the police forestalled me.

Ferrall came down and joined us, and spoke to her at once.

"Good morning, Mrs. Flaherty. Don't you do anything now, but just what you're told to do. And first, tell us a thing or two. How often do you come here? I've seen you in and out, now and again."

"Yes, I do be comin' whin I'm sint for; not of a reg'lar day. Maybe wanst a week, maybe of'ner. Thin agin, not for a fortnight."

"Just as I said," declared Mrs. Reeves. "Vicky often goes away for days at a time."

"Shure she does that. Miss Van Allen is here to-day an' gone to-morrow, but Miss Julie she looks after me wurruk, so she does."

"She engages you when you are needed?" I asked.

"Yes, sir. They's a tillyphone in me husband's shop, an' if anny wan calls me, he lets me know."

"When did they tell you to come here to-day?"

"'Twas yisterday, sir. Miss Julie, she sinds wurrud for me to come this marnin' to clane, as they do be havin' a party last night. Ach, that this thrubble should come!"

"There, now, Mrs. Flaherty, never mind your personal feelings. We're in a hurry." Ferrall was busy making notes of the information he was getting, and I could well understand, that any side-light on Vicky's home life was of importance. So I tarried to listen.

"How long have you worked for Miss Van Allen?"

"A matther av a year or more."

"You clean the rooms upstairs, sometimes?"

"All over the house. Manny's the time I've shwept an' vacuumed Miss Van Allen's own bedroom an' boodore. An' likewise the music room an' parlure an' all. Yis, sor, I'm here frekint."

"What other servants does Miss Van Allen employ?"

"Nobody that lives in, 'ceptin' Miss Julie. But there's the laundry woman, as comes—though more often the wash goes out. Thin, there's a chore boy, as runs arrants; an' sometimes a sewin' woman; an' often the caterer man's dagoes. Yis, an' a boy, a Buttons you know, to open the dure for, say, an afternoon party. You see, Miss Van Allen is off visitin' so much, she don't want steady help."

"Where does she visit?"

"That I dunno. But go, she does, an' I'm thinkin' it's good times she has. For she comes back, chipper an' merry an' glad to see her friends—an' thin, all of a suddint, up an' off agin."

I knew that was Vicky Van's habit. All that the woman said corroborated my idea of the little butterfly's frivolous life. So, why should she keep permanent servants if she was at home only half the time? I knew the troubles Aunt Lucy had with her menials, and I approved of Vicky's wisdom.

"And that explains the empty icebox," Mrs. Reeves was saying, nodding her head in satisfaction. "Vicky meant to go off to-day, after the house was put in order, and she didn't want a lot of food left to spoil."

"Yis, mum," agreed Mrs. Flaherty. "Shall I wash thim dishes now, mum?"

And she was allowed to set to work.

CHAPTER 7: RUTH SCHUYLER

There were many calls on Vicky Van's telephone that morning. It seemed to me that the bell rang almost continually. The police people answered it, and one time, I was surprised to learn that the call was for me.

I took up the receiver and heard Mr. Bradbury's voice.

"I called up your home," he said, "and your sister told me to try this number. Now, look here, Calhoun, I wish you'd go to see Mrs. Schuyler. I've talked with her over the telephone, and she asked me to come up there, but I've got the Crittendon case on this morning, and I can't get away very well. So you go and see what you can do for her. She told me you were there last night, and she's willing to have you in my place."

I agreed, feeling rather flattered that the rich man's widow should so readily accept me as Mr. Bradbury's substitute.

"I'm sorry you're going there," said Mrs. Reeves, her eyes filling with tears, as I took leave of her. "Of course, the Schuylers will pump you about Vicky, and try to make you say that she killed that man!"

"I must tell Mrs. Schuyler the truth," I said.

"Yes, but can't you give Vicky the benefit of the doubt? For there is a doubt. Why should she kill a man she never had seen before?"

"Perhaps he wasn't a stranger to her, after all."

"Why, I heard her say, before he came, that she didn't know him."

"You heard her say she didn't know Mr. Somers," I corrected. "I've been thinking this thing over. Suppose Vicky did know Mr. Schuyler, and when Steele proposed bringing a Mr. Somers—"

"No, you're all wrong!" she exclaimed. "I saw them when they met, and I'm sure they had never laid eyes on each other before. There was not the least sign of recognition. Besides, that isn't like Vicky—to have a millionaire and a married man for her friend. That girl is all right, Mr. Calhoun, and I don't want you to let Mrs. Schuyler think she isn't."

"Perhaps Mrs. Schuyler knows something about her."

"I doubt it. Anyway, you stand up for Vicky, as far as you can do so honestly. Won't you?"

"I can surely promise that," I replied, as I started on my errand.

Approaching the Fifth Avenue residence, I looked at the house, which I had been unable to see clearly the night before.

It was large and handsome, but not one of the most modern mansions. Four stories, it was, and as I glanced up I noticed that all the window shades were down. The floral emblem of death hung at one side of the wide entrance, and as I approached, the door silently swung open.

A footman was in charge, and I was ushered at once to the library where I had been some hours earlier. It was not a cheerful room; the appointments were heavy and somber, though evidently the woods and fabrics were of great value. A shaded electrolier gave a dim light, for the drawn blinds precluded daylight.

A soft step, and Mrs. Schuyler came into the room.

Black garb was not becoming to her. The night before, in her blue house-dress, she had looked almost pretty, but now, in a black gown, without even a bit of relieving white at her throat, she was plain and very pathetic.

Her face was pale and drawn, and her eyes showed dark shadows, as of utter weariness. She greeted me simply and glided to a nearby chair.

"It is kind of you to come, Mr. Calhoun," and the fine quality of her voice and inflection betokened New England ancestry, or training. "As you were here last night—you seem more like a friend than a mere business acquaintance."

"I am very glad, Mrs. Schuyler," and I spoke sincerely, "that you look on me like that. Please tell me anything you wish to, and command me in any way I can serve you."

The speech sounded a little stilted, I knew, but there was something about Ruth Schuyler that called for dignified address. She had the air of bewildered helplessness that always appeals to a man, but she had, too, a look of determination as to one who would do the right thing at any cost of personal unpleasantness.

"It is all so dreadful," she began, and an insuppressible sob threatened her speech. But she controlled it, and went on. "There is so much to be gone through with and I am so ignorant of—of law and—you know—of police doings."

"I understand," I returned, "and anything that you can be spared, rest assured you shall be. But there is much ahead of you that will be hard for you—very hard, and perhaps I can help you get ready for it."

"Will there be an inquest, and all that?" she whispered the word half fearfully.

"Yes, there must be; though not for several days, probably. You know they can't find Miss Van Allen."

"No. Where can she be? I don't suppose they will ever find her. Why should she kill my husband? Have you any theory, Mr. Calhoun? How well did you know this—this person?"

"Only fairly well. By which I mean, I have met her some half a dozen times."

"Always in her own house?"

"Not always. I've attended studio parties where she was present—"

"Oh, Bohemian affairs?"

"Not exactly. Miss Van Allen is a delightful girl, bright and of merry spirits, but in no way fast or of questionable habits."

"That's what they tell me; but pardon me, if I cannot believe a really nice, correct young woman would have a married man visiting her."

"But remember, Mrs. Schuyler, Miss Van Allen did not invite Mr. Schuyler to her house. As near as we can make out, Mr. Steele brought him, without Miss Van Allen's permission. And under an assumed name."

A blush of shame stained her face.

"I realize," she said, "how that reflects against my husband. Must all this be made public, Mr. Calhoun?"

"I fear it must. The law is inexorable in its demands for justice."

"But if they can't find Miss Van Allen, how can they indict her? or whatever the term is. Why can't the whole affair be hushed up? Personally, I would far rather never find the girl—never have her punished, than to drag the Schuyler name through the horrors of a murder trial."

"I quite understand your position, but it will not be possible to evade the legal proceedings. Of course, if Miss Van Allen is never found, the affair must remain a mystery. But she will be found. A lady like that can't drop out of existence."

"No, of course not. Why, her bills must be paid, her household effects looked after; is she in a house or an apartment?"

"A house. I understand she owns it."

"Then she must communicate with her business people—lawyer, bank or creditors. Can't you trace her that way?"

"We hope to. As you say, she must surely return to attend to such matters."

"And her servants? What do they say?"

I described the unusual menage that Vicky Van supported, and Mrs. Schuyler was interested.

"How strange," she said. "She sounds to me like an adventuress!"

"No, she isn't that. She has money enough."

"Where does she get it?"

"I don't know, I'm sure. But she is a quiet, self-reliant little person, and not at all of the adventuress type."

"It doesn't matter," and Mrs. Schuyler sighed. "I don't care anything about her personality. She must be bad or she wouldn't have killed my husband. I'm not defending him, but men don't go to the houses of complete strangers and get murdered by them! And I hope she will never be found, for it might bring out a story of scandal or shame that will always cling to Mr. Schuyler's memory. But, of course, she will come back, and she will plead innocence and lay all blame on Mr. Schuyler. Can't we buy her off? I would pay a large sum to keep her story from the world."

"I'm sorry, Mrs. Schuyler, but that can't be done."

"I thought you would help me—I'm so disappointed."

Tears gathered in her eyes, and her voice trembled. I wished Bradbury had had this job instead of myself, for I am soft-hearted where feminine appeal is concerned, and I didn't know quite what to say.

But just then the two Schuyler sisters came into the library and I rose to greet them.

"Oh," cried Miss Rhoda, "it's all too awful! We can't believe it! I wish I had that girl here! You must find her, Mr. Calhoun—you must!"

"Yes," chimed in Miss Sarah; "she must be brought to judgment. An eye for an eye and a life for a life. That's the Scripture law."

"Don't talk so, Sarah," pleaded Ruth Schuyler. "It won't bring Randolph back, to punish his murderer. And think of the awful publicity!"

"I don't care for that. Murder has been done and murder must be avenged. I'm ashamed of you, Ruth, if you let any idea of personal distaste stand in the way of righteous law and order."

"I, too," agreed Rhoda. "Spare no effort or expense, Mr. Calhoun, to find that wicked girl and have her arrested."

"I daresay you are right," and Mrs. Schuyler's acquiescence showed her to be more or less under the iron hand of the family opinion. "Of course, if you feel that way, I shall raise no obstacle to the law's progress. Whatever you advise, Rhoda, I agree to."

"Certainly you do. You are young, Ruth, and you are not a Schuyler. Why, the very name demands the strongest powers of the law. I only fear that the most desperate efforts may not succeed. What is your opinion, Mr. Calhoun? Can they find that woman?"

The scorn of the last two words, as uttered by Rhoda Schuyler's sharp tongue, is not to be reproduced in print.

"I think most probably, yes, Miss Schuyler. I think she must return sooner or later."

"Don't wait for that!" exclaimed Sarah. "Send people to search for her. Scour the country. Don't let her get away beyond retrieval. Offer a reward, if necessary, but get her!"

"A reward!" repeated Rhoda. "Yes, that's it. Put it in the paper at once; a large reward for any information of Miss Van Allen."

"Stay," I urged; "don't decide on such measures too hastily. Might you not defeat your own purpose? Miss Van Allen doubtless will see the papers, wherever she may be. If she learns of the reward, she will hide herself more securely than ever."

"I think so, too," said Ruth, in her gentle voice. "I am sure, Rhoda, we oughtn't to do anything like that just yet. Oh, how hard it is to know what to do."

"Yes, we've always deferred everything to Randolph. How can we get along without him?"

"We must," and Mrs. Schuyler set her pale lips together in an evident determination to be brave and strong. "Now, Mr. Calhoun, what is there to be discussed in a business way? I mean regarding Mr. Schuyler's business with you or Mr. Bradbury?"

"Nothing at present," I returned, feeling sure the poor woman had quite enough on her mind. "The will can be examined at your convenience, and any questions of securities or money can rest over for a time. Do you wish any ready cash? Or shall we look after any money matters?"

"Thank you, no. Such things are systematically arranged in the household. Jepson attends to bills and tradesmen. My greatest wish is for a secretary or some person to write notes and look after the flood of letters and telegrams that has already begun."

I felt surprised, for I had assumed that the rich man's wife had a social secretary of her own.

"I've no one," she said, in response to my glance, "Mr. Schuyler didn't wish me to have a secretary, and indeed I didn't need one. But now—"

"Of course, it is necessary now."

"Not at all," interrupted Miss Rhoda. "I am surprised at you, Ruth! You know how Randolph objected to such things, and now, as soon as he is gone, you begin to—"

"Hush, Rhoda," said Ruth, with gentle dignity. "It was not necessary before, but it is now. You've no idea what a task it will be. All our friends and many of Randolph's acquaintances will call or send messages and they must be acknowledged—"

"And, pray, what else have you to do, but acknowledge them? Sarah and I will attend to our own. A great many, doubtless, but not too much of a task for us, when it is in memory of our dear brother!"

"Very well," and Ruth spoke calmly, "we will wait for a day or two, Mr. Calhoun, and then, if, as I believe, the matter requires further consideration, we will discuss it again."

Clever woman, I thought to myself. She isn't altogether chummy with those old maid sisters, and yet she knows better than to have any open disagreement. I'll bet she gets her secretary when she gets ready for one! I'll be on the lookout for the right girl for her.

"When will they bring my husband home?" she continued, without waiting for comment on her decision about the secretary.

"Some time to-day," I returned, looking commiseratingly at the harassed white face. "Probably this afternoon. Can I take any message regarding the funeral arrangements?"

"Not yet," and Ruth Schuyler shuddered. "Those details are so terrible—"

"Terrible, yes," said Miss Sarah, "but they must be looked after. We will see the undertaker's men, Ruth. I think Rhoda and I will know better what is fit and proper for Randolph's burial ceremonies than you possibly can."

I began to realize that the sisters had a family pride which did not include their brother's wife in their councils. Apparently she was, or they deemed her, of lesser birth or social standing. Personally, however, I greatly preferred the gentle kindliness of the widow to the aristocratic hauteur of the sisters.

Ruth Schuyler made no objection to the proposition, and seemed relieved that her advice would not be required.

"Who is in the house where Mr. Schuyler was—where he died?" she asked, hesitatingly.

"Only the police," I answered, "unless Miss Van Allen has returned."

"Were—were there many people there—last night?"

Clearly, she wanted to know more details of the occasion, but didn't like to show curiosity.

"Yes," I informed her, "quite a number. It was Miss Van Allen's birthday, and so, a sort of little celebration."

"Her birthday? How old was she?"

"I've no idea. I should guess about twenty-two or twenty-three."

"Is she—is—what does she look like?"

The eternal feminine wanted to ask "is she pretty?" but Ruth Schuyler's dignity scarcely permitted the question. I noticed, too, that the sisters listened attentively for my reply.

"Yes," I said, truthfully, "she is pretty. She is small, with very black hair, and large, dark gray eyes. She is exceedingly chic and up-to-date as to costumes, and is of vivacious and charming manner."

"Humph!" sniffed Miss Rhoda, "an actress?"

"Not at all! Victoria Van Allen is a well-bred lady if there ever was one."

"You are a staunch friend, Mr. Calhoun," and Mrs. Schuyler looked her surprise.

"I speak only as I feel; I can't say surely that Miss Van Allen did not commit this crime, for I know there is evidence against her. But I can't reconcile the deed with her character, as I know it, and I, for one, shall wait further developments before I condemn her. But, of course, Mrs. Schuyler, my personal feelings in the matter have no weight in law, and I stand ready to obey whatever orders you may give in connection with a search for the missing girl."

"I don't know exactly what I do want done, yet, Mr. Calhoun," and Ruth Schuyler glanced deferringly toward the sisters.

"No, we don't." For once Sarah agreed with Ruth. "After the funeral, we can set our minds to the finding of the criminal. Of course, the police will do all they can, meantime, to trace her?"

"Of course. And such a plan is best. She may return-"

"To a house guarded by police?" asked Ruth.

"Possibly. If she is innocent, why not?"

"Innocent!" exclaimed Miss Rhoda with utmost scorn.

"Some of her friends think her so," I observed. "Mrs. Reeves, a lady who was at the party, stayed in the house all night, and is, I think, there still."

"Why did she do that?" asked Mrs. Schuyler, looking puzzled.

"She hoped Miss Van Allen would return, and she waited there to look after her."

"That was kind. Who is this lady?"

"She lives down on Washington Square. I only know her slightly, but she is a warm-hearted and a most capable and sensible one. She refuses to believe that Vicky Van—"

"What do you call her?"

"Her friends call her Vicky Van. It—it sort of suits her."

"From what you say, I judge she is not the terror I thought her at first; but, all the same, she murdered my husband, and I cannot look on her as you seem to."

"Nor can I blame you. Your feelings toward her are entirely just, Mrs. Schuyler."

CHAPTER 8: THE LETTER-BOX

"It's a queer case," said Mr. Bradbury to me, when I reached the office that afternoon. "Of course, I know Randolph Schuyler was no saint, but I never supposed he was deep enough in any affair to have a woman kill him. And so near his own home, too! He might have had the decency to choose his lady acquaintances in more remote sections of the city."

"That isn't the queerest part to me," I returned. "What I can't understand is, why that girl stabbed him. She didn't know him—"

"Now, now, Calhoun, she must have known him. She didn't know any Somers, we'll say, but she must have known Schuyler. A murder has to have a motive. She had provided herself with that knife beforehand, you see, and she got him out to the dining-room purposely."

"I can't think it," I said, and I sighed. "I know Vicky Van fairly well, and she wouldn't—"

"You can't say what a woman would or wouldn't do. But it's not our business to look after the criminal part of it, we've got all we can handle, attending to the estate. And here's another thing. I wish you'd do all that's necessary up at the house. I always got along all right with Randolph Schuyler, but I can't stand those sisters of his. His wife I have never met. But those old Schuyler women get on my nerves. So you look after them. You're more of a ladies' man than I am, so you go there and talk pretty when they want legal advice."

"I'm willing," I agreed. "I don't care such a lot for the sisters myself, but Mrs. Schuyler is a young thing, ignorant of her own rights, and those old maids boss her like fury. I'm going to see that she has her own way in some few things, at least. She inherits half the fortune, you know."

"Yes, and the sisters a quarter each. That is, after some minor bequests and charitable donations are settled. Schuyler was a good sort—as men go."

"Then men go pretty badly! He was a brute to his wife; I've been told he ruled her with a rod of iron, and what he didn't bother her about, the old sisters did."

"That's neither here nor there. Don't you try to be a peacemaker in that family. I know those two old ladies, and they'd resent anything in the way of criticism of their treatment of their sister-in-law. And, if Schuyler didn't treat his wife handsomely, she's rid of him now, at any rate."

"You're a cold-blooded thing, Bradbury," I informed him, "and I am going to do all I can for that young widow. She'll have a lot of unpleasant publicity at best, and if I can shield her from part of it, so much the better."

"All right, Calhoun. Do what you like, but don't get in on the detective work. I know your weakness for that sort of thing, and I know if you begin, you'll never let up."

Bradbury was right. I have a fondness for detective work—not the police part of it, but the inquiry into mystery, the deduction from clues and the sifting of evidence. I had no mind to miss the inquest, and I had a burning curiosity to know what had become of Vicky Van. This was not only curiosity, either. I had a high respect and a genuine liking for that little lady, and, as Mrs. Reeves had put it, I was only too willing to give her the benefit of the doubt.

Though I couldn't feel any real doubt that she had killed Schuyler. As Bradbury said, she didn't know a Mr. Somers, but she may have known the millionaire Schuyler. I had never seen anything of a seamy side to Vicky's character; but then, I didn't know her so very well, and the man was dead, and who else could have killed him?

I went around to the caterer's on my way uptown that afternoon, and asked him as to the reliability of Luigi and the probable truth of his story.

"That man," Fraschini told me, "is as honest as the day. I've had him longer than any of my other waiters, and he has never said or done anything to make me doubt his accuracy. I believe, Mr. Calhoun, that Luigi saw exactly what he said he saw."

"Might he not have been mistaken in the identity of the woman?"

"Not likely. I'll call him, and you can question him."

This was what I wanted, to question the waiter alone, and I welcomed the opportunity.

"I know it was Miss Van Allen," was the quiet response of the Italian to my inquiry. "I cannot be mistaken. I had seen her many times during the evening. I, therefore, recognized the gown she wore, of light yellow gauzy stuff and an over-dress of long gold bead fringes. I saw her stand above the fallen body, looking down at it with a horrified face. I saw stains of blood on her gown—"

"Where?" I interrupted. "What part of her gown?"

Luigi thought a moment. "On the lower flounces, as if her skirts had brushed against the—the victim, when she stooped over him."

"Did she herself observe these stains?"

"Yes; she looked at them, and looked frightened and then she ran to the hall."

"And you saw no other person near?"

"None."

"And heard nobody?"

"I heard only the voices from the parlor. There was much noise of laughter and talk there."

No amount of questioning could change or add to Luigi's story. It was quite evident that he was telling just what he saw, and had no interest in coloring it to make it appear different in any way. He admired Miss Van Allen, he said she was a pleasant lady and not hard to please if her orders were faithfully carried out. He expressed no personal interest in the question of her guilt or innocence, he simply told what he had seen. I didn't altogether like his stolid indifference, it seemed impossible there should be so little humanity in a fellow-being, but I knew he was a good and conscientious waiter, and I concluded he was nothing more.

I went home, and, of course, was met by Aunt Lucy and Winnie with a perfect storm of questions.

"After dinner," I begged. "Let me get a little rest and food, and then I'll tell you all I know."

But after a few spoonfuls of soup, Winnie declared I was too nervous to eat and I might as well talk.

"Well, I will," I said. "But, look here, you two. To begin with, I want you to understand that I'm involved in this matter in a business way, and I'm also interested in a personal way. And I don't want any silly talk about it's being unfortunate or regrettable that I should be. It's a business case, Aunt Lucy, as far as the settlement of Mr. Schuyler's estate is concerned, and it's a personal affair that I'm acquainted with Miss Van Allen; and I propose to make more or less effort to find some trace of that girl, and to see if there is any possible chance that she may not be the guilty one after all."

"Good for you, Lord Chesterton!" cried Winnie. "I always knew you were the soul of chivalry, and now you're proving it! What are you going to do—to find out things, I mean?"

"I don't know yet, Win. But if you want to help me, you can do a lot."

"Indeed, she won't!" declared Aunt Lucy. "If you have to do these things as a matter of business, I can't object. But I won't have Winnie dragged into it."

"No dragging, Aunt Lu, and nothing very desperate for Winnie to do. But, I'd be jolly glad if both of you would just glance out of the window occasionally and see if you see anything going on at the Van Allen house, that's all."

"Oh, I'll do that!" Winnie cried. "Nobody can see me, I'll keep behind our curtains, and I can see that house perfectly well."

"I don't mean all the time, child. But I do feel sure that Vicky Van will come back there, and if you glance out now and then, you might see her go in or out."

"But it's dark," said Aunt Lucy, who was becoming interested, in spite of her scruples.

"I don't mean to-night, or any night. But in the daytime. She's likely to come, if at all, in broad daylight, I think."

"Aren't the police keeping guard on the house?" inquired my aunt.

"Only the regular patrolman. He passes it every few hours, joggles the doorknob, and goes on. If Vicky is as clever as I think she is, she'll time that policeman, and sneak into the house between his rounds. It's only a chance, you know, but you might see her."

And then I told them all I knew myself of the whole affair. And seeing that I was deeply into the turmoil of it all, and had grave responsibilities, Aunt Lucy withdrew all objections and sympathized with me. Also, she was impressed with my important business connections with the Schuyler family, and was frankly curious about that aristocratic household. I was asked over and over again as to their mode of living, the furniture and appointments of the house, and the attitudes of the widow and the sisters toward each other.

It was late in the evening before I remembered some important papers Mr. Bradbury had given me to hand to Mrs. Schuyler, and as soon as I thought of them I telephoned to know if I might then bring them over.

"Yes," came back Ruth Schuyler's soft voice. "I wish you would. I want to consult you about some other things also."

The interview was less trying than that of the morning had been. Several matters of inheritance, insurance, and such things were discussed, and Mrs. Schuyler was more composed and calm.

She looked better, too, though this was doubtless due, in part, to the fact that she wore a white house dress which was far more becoming than black to her colorless face and light hair.

"I don't know," she said, at length, "whether what I want to say should be said to you or to the detective."

"Tell me first," I said, "and I may be able to advise you. In any case, it will be confidential."

"You are kind," she said, and her grateful eyes smiled appreciatively. "It's this. I'd rather not have that—that Miss Van Allen traced, if it can be prevented in any way. I have a special reason for this, which I think I will tell you. It is, that, on thinking it over I have become convinced that my husband must have known the young woman, and the acquaintance was not to his credit. For some reason, I think, she must have forbidden him the house, and that is why he went there under an assumed name. Mr. Lowney succeeded in getting Mr. Steele on the long distance telephone—"

"Why, where is Steele?"

"In Chicago. Mr. Lowney says that he had to go there on the midnight train, and that is why he left the lady's house—Miss Van Allen's house, so suddenly."

"Really? Well, I am surprised. But, go on, what else did Steele say?"

"He said that Mr. Schuyler was with him at the club, and that he, Mr. Steele, said he was going to Miss Van Allen's party and Mr. Schuyler begged him to take him along, and introduce him as Mr. Somers. It seems he had asked Mr. Steele before to do this, but this time he was more insistent. So Mr. Steele did it. Of course, Mr. Calhoun, I asked Mr. Lowney minutely about all this, because I want to know just what circumstances led up to my husband's going to that house."

"Of course, Mrs. Schuyler, you have every right to know. And did Steele say that was Mr. Schuyler's first visit there or merely his first visit as Mr. Somers?"

"Mr. Steele thought Mr. Schuyler had never been to the house before at all. But may he not have been mistaken? May not Mr. Schuyler have known the lady previously—oh, it is such a moil! But, in any case, Mr. Calhoun, it seems to me that further probing and searching will only pile up opprobrium on the name of Schuyler, and—I can't stand it. I am so unused to notoriety or publicity I can't face all the unpleasantness that must follow! Do help me to avoid it, won't you?"

"I certainly will, if I can. But I fear you ask the impossible, Mrs. Schuyler. The law will not be stopped in its course by personal inclinations."

"No, I suppose not. What is it, Tibbetts?"

The last question was addressed to her maid, who appeared at the doorway. The sad-faced woman looked at her mistress with a mingled air of deference and commiseration.

"The telephone, ma'am," she said. "I said you were busily engaged, but it is some young woman who begs to speak to you a moment."

Mrs. Schuyler excused herself and left the room, and Tibbetts, smoothing down her trim white apron, followed.

"Another would-be secretary," my hostess said, as she returned. "I don't know how a report that I wanted one travelled so quickly, but I've had three offered since noon."

"Do the Schuyler ladies still object?"

"No; at least, they are willing. But I don't want any except a capable one. Not so much experienced, as quick-witted and intelligent. You may as well know, Mr. Calhoun, since you are to look after my affairs, that my late husband was of strictly plain habits. He was almost frugal in his ideas of how little womankind should be indulged in any luxuries or unnecessary comforts. This did not incommode his sisters for they were of the same mind. But I desired certain things which he saw fit to deny me. I make no complaint, I bear his memory no ill will, but I feel that now I may have some of these things. I am my own mistress, and while I have no wish to cast any reflection on Mr. Schuyler's management of his own house, yet, it is now my house, and I must have the privilege of ordering it as I choose."

It had come already, then. Ruth Schuyler and her Puritanical sisters-in-law had met the issue, and Ruth had stood up for her rights. I felt that I knew the woman well enough to know she would not have taken this stand so soon after her husband's death except that some discussion or disagreement had made it necessary for her to assert herself. I bowed in acquiescence, and said, "I am sure, Mrs. Schuyler, there can be no objection to your doing exactly as you please. This house is entirely your own, half Mr. Schuyler's fortune is yours, and you are responsible to nobody for your actions. If not intrusive, I will offer to look you up a suitable secretary. I have a young woman in mind, whom I think you would like."

"I am not easy to please," she said, smiling a little; "I have a very definite idea of what I want. Who is your friend?"

"Not a friend, exactly. An acquaintance of my sister's, who is eligible for the post, if she suits you. Shall I send her round to see you to-morrow?"

"Yes, please. Your mention of her is enough recommendation. I want, Mr. Calhoun, to do more or less charitable work this winter. That was another of Mr. Schuyler's whims, to attend to all charities himself, and to object to my giving anything personally. As I shall be quiet and unoccupied this winter, I plan to do some systematic work in a benevolent way. I know this sounds strange to you, that I should be planning these things so soon. But the truth is, I do plan them, purposely, because I don't want to think about the present horror. I need something to keep my mind from thinking of the awful tragedy or I shall go mad. It seemed to me not wrong to think about some work that should benefit others; and to do this, will give me an outlet for my energies and be helpful to the poor and suffering."

Ruth Schuyler looked almost beautiful as her face glowed with enthusiasm on her subject. I realized how the nervous, highstrung woman must be torn with agony at the revelations of her husband's defects and the uncertainty of his honor and morality, and all in addition to the terrible experiences she was undergoing and must yet encounter.

I went home filled with a desire to help her in every way I could, and though I went to my room at once, I could not think of sleep. I felt like planning ways to put the police off the track or finding some method of making them cease their hunt for Vicky Van.

I went down to the library, and sat down for a smoke and a revery. And I sat there until very late, after two o'clock, in fact, without getting any nearer a plan than I was at the start.

It was nearly three, when I concluded that I could sleep at last. I stood by the front window a moment, looking over at Vicky Van's house, across the street, and a few doors from our own.

As I looked at the darkened dwelling, I saw the front door slowly open. There was no one outside, it was being opened from inside. As I knew the body of Mr. Schuyler had been taken away, and the house had been deserted by all who had been there, and that it was in custody of the police, I looked curiously to see what would happen next.

Out of the door came a slight, small figure. It was, I felt positive, Vicky Van herself! I couldn't mistake that sleek, black head—she wore no hat—or those short, full skirts, that she always wore. She looked about cautiously, and then with swift motions she unlocked the letter-box that was beside her front door, took out several letters, relocked the box and slipped back into the house again! Without stopping to think I opened my front door, and flew across the street. Mounting her steps, I rang the doorbell hard. There was no response, and I kept on ringing—a veritable bombardment. Then the door opened a very little bit—I could see it was on a night-chain—and Vicky's voice said, "Please go away."

"No, I won't," I said, "let me come in."

"I can't let you come in. Go away, please."

And then the door closed, in my very face, and though I pleaded, "Vicky, do let me in!" there was no response.

CHAPTER 9: THE SOCIAL SECRETARY

I stood staring at the closed door. What did it mean? Why was Vicky in there and why wouldn't she let me come in?

Then, as I collected my wits, I laughed at myself. I knew why she was there—to get her mail. Doubtless there were important letters that she must have, and she had dared discovery to come at dead of night to get them. The patrolman was not in sight. She had looked out for this, of course. It was the merest chance that I had seen her, otherwise she would have escaped all observation. At three in the morning there are almost no people abroad in the quieter streets of the city, and Vicky had timed her visit well. Of course, she had her own keys, and I felt sure she had stealthily entered at the basement door, and waited her time to secure the letters from the mail-box.

I looked at the mail-box, an unusual appendage to a private residence, but Vicky was away from home so much, it was doubtless necessary. I tried to look in at a window, but all shades were down and there were no lights inside. I wanted to ring the doorbell again, but a sense of delicacy forbade me. I was not a detective, and if I persisted, I might attract the attention of a passer-by or of the returning policeman, and so get Vicky into all sorts of trouble. I wasn't tracking the girl down. If she was a criminal, let the police find her, I had no desire to aid their efforts, but I did want to see Vicky Van. I wanted to offer her my help—not in escaping justice, exactly—but I wondered if I mightn't do some little errands or favors that would show my friendliness.

I went slowly toward home, when I had an inspiration. Hastening into my own house, I flew to the telephone and called Vicky's number, which I knew well.

I waited some time for a response, but at last I heard Vicky's voice say, "Who is it, please?"

An impulse of protection for her, not for myself, led me to withhold my name. Nor did I speak hers.

I said, "This is the man who just left your house. I called up to offer help, if I can render you any."

"That's good of you," she returned, in a heartfelt way. "I appreciate such kindness, but you can do nothing— nothing, thank you."

"At least, talk to me a few minutes. I'm so anxious about you. You are not implicated in the—in the matter, are you?"

"Don't ask me," she murmured, in such a serious voice, that my heart sank. "What I did—or didn't do— must always remain a mystery. I cannot tell you— anything. Don't ask. And, if you would help me, try your best to have inquiries stopped. Can you do this?"

"I fear not. But can't I see you—somewhere—and we can talk plainly?"

"Do you want to?"

"Indeed I do."

"Then you do believe in me? Do you hold me blameless?"

I hesitated at this. I couldn't lie to her, nor could I rid my mind of the conviction of her guilt I said, "I will, if you assure me that is the truth."

"I—I can't do that—good-bye."

"Wait a minute. Did you know the expected guest was coming under an assumed name?"

"I did not."

"Did you know any Somers?"

"No."

"Did you know—the real man?"

"I had met him once, at a dance."

"Did you like him?"

"I neither liked nor disliked. He was an object of utter indifference to me."

"Then why did you—"

"Hush! You can never know. I can't tell you—"

"Then don't. Please believe I want to befriend you."
The agony and fear in Vicky's voice thrilled me, and I
desired only to shield and protect her. She was so young
and alone.

"It is good to have a friendly voice speak to me. But
you can only forget me."

"No, let me do something definite. Some errand of
trust, some matter of confidence—"

"Do you mean it? Will you?"

"Gladly! What is it?"

"Then if you will collect my mail from the box at the
door, after a few days—say, three days—and put it aside
for me. You saw me get it to-night, I suppose, and it is a
dangerous thing for me to do."

"Where are you—I mean, where are you staying?"

"Don't ask. I am safe. I see the newspapers and I
know I am to be hunted down. So I must hide. I cannot
face the inquiries—I fear arrest and—and punishment—"

Her tones betrayed guilty fear, and I shuddered at the
confirmation of my suspicions. But I would do what I
could for her.

"How shall I get your letters?" I asked, and I honestly
tried not to disclose my sudden knowledge of her guilt.
But her quick ears caught my changed inflection.

"You believe me guilty!" she said, and she stifled a
sob. "Yet, still, you will help me! God bless you! Listen,
then, for I must stop this talking, it is too desperately
dangerous. I will leave the key of the mail box—no, I will
send it to you by mail, that will be the safest. Then will
you get the letters and put them—where shall I say?"

"I'll mail them to you."

"No, that would never do. You can get into this house,
can't you? The police will let you in at any time?"

"Yes, I can probably manage that."

"Then bring them with you, all of the three days' mail
at once, you understand, and put them in that great

Chinese jar, in the music room. The one with the gold dragon on the cover. No one will look there for them. I will manage to come and get them very soon. Please don't spy on me, will you, Chester?"

The use of my first name was, I knew, inadvertent and unconscious. It thrilled me. There was a marvellous fascination always about Vicky Van, and now, at the end of this my mysterious night telephone conversation, I felt its thrill and I agreed to her plea.

"No, dear," I said, and not till afterward did I realize the term I had used, "I will not spy. But promise me that you will call on me for any help you may need. And tell me—are you alone or is Julie with you?"

"Julie is with me," she returned. "She helps protect me, and with your friendship, too, I am blessed indeed. But this is good-bye. I shall leave New York in a few days never to return. I must have that mail, or I would go at once. If you will help me get that, you will do all there is left for any one to do for me in the world."

Her tone frightened me. "Vicky!" I cried, forgetting all caution. "Don't—my dear, don't—" but I could not put in words the fear that had suddenly come to me, and even as I stammered for speech, the click came that told me she had hung up the receiver.

I cursed myself for my stupidity in speaking her name. Such a blunder! Why, it might have been overheard by anybody on the line. No wonder she left me. Doubtless I had driven her from her house.

I flew to the window. Then I remembered I had promised not to spy, and I turned quickly away. If she were about to disappear silently and stealthily from that house, I must not know it.

I went to my room, but not to sleep. Clearly, I was not to know untroubled slumber again very soon. I sat up and thought it all over.

How strange that I should have "spied" on her just at the moment she was secretly getting her letters. But, I realized, I had looked at the house so often it would be stranger still if I had missed her!

And she was to send me her box key, and I was to secrete her letters for her. Important indeed, those letters must be, that she should go to such lengths to get them. Well, I had constituted myself her knight errant in that particular, and I would fulfil the trust.

Beneath the thrilling excitement of the night's occurrence, I felt a dull, sad foreboding. All Vicky had said or done pointed to guilt. Had she been innocent, she would have told me so, by word or by implication. She would have given me a tacit assurance of her guiltlessness, or would have cried out at the injustice of suspicion.

But none of these things entered into her talk, or even into her voice or intonations. She had sounded sad, hopeless, despairing. And her last words made me fear she contemplated taking her own life.

Poor little Vicky Van. Light-hearted, joy-loving Vicky. What was the mystery back of it all? What could it be? Well, at least, I would scrupulously perform the task she had set me, and I would do it well. I knew I could manage to get into the house by making up some story for the police. But I must wait for the promised key.

With a glimmer of hope that the mailed parcel containing the key might give me a clue to Vicky's whereabouts, I at last went to sleep.

Next morning at breakfast I said nothing of my night experiences. I told Winnie, however, that she needn't watch the Van Allen house, as I had heard that Vicky had left it permanently.

"However could you hear that?" exclaimed my wideawake sister. "Have you had a wireless from the fugitive?"

"Something of the sort," I said, smilingly. "And now, listen here, Win. How do you think that friend of yours,

Miss Crowell, would like to be a social secretary for Mrs. Schuyler?"

"She'd love it!" cried Winnie. "Does Mrs. Schuyler want one?"

"Yes, and she wants her mighty quick. From what you've said of the Crowell girl, I should think she'd be just the one. Can you get her on the telephone?"

"Yes, but not so early as this. I'll call her about ten."

"All right, you fix it up. I expect Mrs. Schuyler will pay proper salary to the right secretary. Of course, Miss Crowell is experienced?"

"Oh, yes," assured Win, "and I'm sure she'll love to go. Why, any secretary would be glad to go there."

"Not just now, I should think," observed Aunt Lucy. "The amount of work there must be something fearful."

"It will be heavy, for a time," I agreed, "but it is only for Mrs. Schuyler's personal correspondence and business. I mean, the other two ladies would not expect to use her services."

"All right," said Winnie, "I'll fix it up with Edith Crowell, and if she can't go, I'll ask her to recommend somebody. Shall I send her there to-day?"

"Yes, as soon as she will go. And let me know— telephone the office about noon."

"Yep," Winnie promised, and I went away, my head in a whirl with the various and sundry matters I had to attend to.

I don't think I thought of the secretary matter again, until at noon, Winnie telephoned me that it was all right. I thanked her, and promptly forgot the episode.

And so it was, that when I reached home that night, I had one of the surprises of my life.

Winnie came to dinner, smiling, and rather excited-looking.

"What's up, Infant?" I asked. "Have you accepted a proposal from a nice college lad?"

"Huh!" and Win's head tossed. "I guess you'll open your eyes when I tell you what I have accepted!"

"Tell it out, Angel Child. Relieve your own impatience."

"Well, if you please, I have accepted the post of social secretary to Mrs. Randolph Schuyler."

"Winifred Elizabeth Calhoun! You haven't!"

"I thought I'd arouse some slight interest," she said, and she calmly went on with her dinner.

I looked at Aunt Lucy, who sat with a resigned expression, toying with her unused oyster-fork.

"What does she mean?" I asked.

"She has done just what she says," replied Aunt Lucy. "But only for a few days. Miss Crowell—"

"Let me tell!" interrupted Winnie. "It's my party! You see, Chet, Edith Crowell is wild to have the place, and is going to take it, but she can't go until the first of next week. And she doesn't want to lose the chance, so I went over and told Mrs. Schuyler about it. And then as she was simply swamped with letters and telegrams and telephones and callers, and goodness knows what all, I offered to help her out till Edith can get there. And she was so grateful—oh, I think she is a darling. I never saw anyone I liked and admired so much at first sight."

"She is charming," I conceded, "but what a crazy scheme, Win! How did you persuade Aunt Lucy to agree?"

"I managed her," and Winnie bobbed her wise young head, cannily.

It came to me in a moment. Though not exactly a tuft hunter, Aunt Lucy was deeply impressed by real grandeur and elegance. And it came to me at once, that Winnie's tales of the great house and the aristocratic people, had a strong influence on our aunt's views and had brought about her permission for Win to go there for a few days. And it was no harm. It wasn't as if Winnie were a regular secretary, but just to hold the place for Miss Crowell, was simply a kindly deed.

And so, after dinner, I settled myself in our cosy library for a comfortable smoke, and bade Winnie tell me every single thing that had happened through the day.

"Oh, it was thrilling!" Winnie exclaimed. "Part of the time I was at the desk in the library, and part of the time upstairs in Mrs. Schuyler's very own room. She was so kind to me, but she is nearly distracted and I don't wonder! The undertakers' men were in and out, and those two old maids—his sisters, you know—were everlastingly appearing and disappearing. And they don't like Mrs. Schuyler an awful lot, nor she them. Oh, they're polite and all that, but you can see they're of totally different types. I like Mrs. Schuyler heaps better, but still, there's something about the old girls that's the real thing. They're Schuylers and also they're Salton-stalls, and farther back, I believe they're Cabots or something."

"And Mrs. Schuyler, what is she?" I asked, as Win paused for breath.

"I don't know. Nothing particular, I guess. Oh, yes, I learned her name was Ellison before she was married, but the sisters don't consult her about family matters at all. They do about clothes, though. And she knows a lot. Why, Chess, she's having the loveliest things made, if they are mourning, and the sisters, they ask her about everything they order—to wear, I mean. And, just think! Mrs. Schuyler never wears any jewels but pearls! It's a whim, you know, or it was her husband's whim, or something, but anyway, she has oceans of pearls, and no other gems at all."

"Did she tell you so?"

"Yes; but it came in the conversation, you know. She is no boaster. No sir-ee! She's the modestest, gentlest, sweetest little lady I ever saw. I just love her! Well, I answered a lot of letters for her, and she liked the way I did it, and she liked me, I guess, for she said she only hoped Miss Crowell would suit her as well."

"She knows you're my sister?"

"Of course. But that isn't why she likes me, old bunch of conceit! Though, I must admit, she likes you, Chet. She said you were not only kind, but you have a fair amount of intelligence—no, she didn't use those words, exactly, but I gathered that was what she meant. The funeral is to be tomorrow evening, you know. I had to write and telephone quite a good deal about that, though the sisters tended to it mostly."

"Was there much said about—about the actual case—Winnie?"

"You mean about the murder?" Win's clear eyes didn't blink at the word; "no, not much in my hearing. But Mrs. Schuyler wasn't in the room all the time. And I know Mr. Lowney—isn't he the detective?—was there once, and I think, twice."

"Did you see anyone else?"

"Only some of the servants. Mrs. Schuyler's own maid, her name is Tibbetts, is the sort you read about in English novels. A nice, motherly woman, with gray hair and a black silk apron. I liked her, but the maid who looks after the old sisters, I didn't like so well."

"Never mind the maids, tell me more about Mrs. Schuyler. Does she think Vicky Van killed Mr. Schuyler? Since you're in this thing so deep Win, there's no use mincing matters."

"I should say not! Yes, of course, she thinks the Vicky person did the killing. How could she think anything else? And the two sisters are madly revengeful. As soon as the funeral is over, they're going to work to find that girl and bring her to justice! They say the inquest will help a lot. When will that be, Chess? Can I go to it?"

"No, of course not, Winnie?" This from Aunt Lucy. "It's one thing for you to help Mrs. Schuyler out in an emergency, but you're not to get mixed up in a murder trial!"

"An inquest isn't a trial, Auntie," and Win looked like a wise owl, as she aired her new and suddenly acquired knowledge. "Can't I go, Chess?"

"We'll see, Infant. Perhaps, if Mrs. Schuyler needs your services she may want you there with her."

"Oh, in that case—" began Aunt Lucy, but Winnie was off again on one of her enthusiastic descriptions of the grand ways of the Schuyler household, and Aunt Lucy was quite willing to listen.

As for me, I wanted the benefit of every possible sidelight on the whole business, and I, too, took in all Winnie's detailed narrations.

CHAPTER 10: THE INQUEST

The inquest was in progress. In the coroner's courtroom inquiry was being made in an endeavor to discover who was responsible for the death of Randolph Schuyler. The funeral of the millionaire had taken place, and the will had been read, and now the public awaited news of the action of the police in placing the crime and producing the criminal.

The case had become a celebrated one, not only because of the prominence of the victim, but because of the mystery surrounding the young woman suspected of the deed of murder.

Many voluntary witnesses had come forward with additional information regarding Victoria Van Allen, but none of these knew anything more of her relatives or progenitors than I did myself.

Some of these were asked to testify at the inquest, but more were not so called on, as their testimony was in no way material or vital.

I did not propose to attend all the sessions, myself, but I wanted to hear the opening queries and learn just how the case was to be managed.

Doctor Remson told of his examination of Mr. Schuyler's body and testified that death was practically instantaneous as a result of a single stab of the short, sharp knife. The knife was produced and identified. It had been carefully taken care of and had been photographed to preserve the faint fingermarks, which were on its handle, and which might or might not be the prints of the murderer's fingers.

The caterer Fraschini told of his orders for the party supper, and of the sending of his best and most faithful waiters to attend to the feast.

Luigi, the head waiter, again went over his story. I had heard this twice before, but I listened with deep interest, and I realized, that, granting the truth of his recital, there was no room for doubt of Vicky Van's guilt.

I hadn't of course, told of seeing her take her mail from the box that night, nor of her talking to me over the telephone. Should absolute law and justice call for that information, I might give it up, but at present, I was awaiting developments.

Vicky had sent me her mailbox key, and I had received it duly, by mail. It was not sent by parcel post, nor was it registered—these would have called for the sender's address—but, sent by ordinary first-class letter post, the flat little key came duly and promptly.

I had not used it yet, the time was not ripe until that same night, and I intended to say nothing of it, until I had fulfilled my promise, if, indeed, I ever told of it.

But Luigi's story as I heard it again made me shiver with apprehension. Surely, since he saw Vicky right there at the moment, bending over the victim, blood stains on her gown, there could be no loophole of innocence. Had the murderer been some one else, and had Vicky known it, she must have made an outcry—must have accused the guilty party. There was no one whom Vicky loved well enough to wish to shield. And, too, the guests were all in the big living-room; there was no one unaccounted for. If Luigi himself, or any of the caterer's men had by chance done the deed, Vicky wouldn't have run away! There was no sense in that. So I could see no possible theory but that of Vicky's actual guilt. Why she did it, was another story. She may have known Schuyler before, might have known him a long time, might have had her own reasons for wishing him dead; but all that was outside the issue of her criminality. There was no eyewitness of the stabbing itself, but Luigi's presence on the scene an instant later, left no room for question as to the hand that had held the knife.

The jury seemed to think this. Gravely the men listened to what the Italian told, and their faces showed what they believed.

Then came the guests of the party. One after another, they told the same story. All knew Vicky fairly well, as a pleasant acquaintance; all liked her as a good friend; all enjoyed her as a delightful hostess; and many told individual instances of Vicky's kind heart and helping hand. Not infrequently had she lent assistance, both financial and in other ways, to these friends of hers. Never, they all said, had they known her to do a mean or deceitful act or to say an unkind or malicious word.

The men spoke of her as a gay, light-hearted butterfly girl, who was a coquette, but who stopped short of a real flirtation; the women gave her such commendation as is rarely given them to their own sex, and declared that Miss Van Allen was a simple, kindly, generous nature without a trace of the disposition which causes a woman to be dubbed a cat.

Norman Steele was present. He explained his sudden departure from the party by the fact that he had to catch an owl train for Chicago. He said, further, that Randolph Schuyler had asked him to take him around to Vicky Van's, as he wanted to meet her. But he had asked Steele, especially, to introduce him as Mr. Somers. He had given no reason for this, and Steele had thought little of it. Randolph Schuyler was a man whom his friends obeyed, often without question. I understood this. Steele was no more of a toady to the millionaire than most men would be; but a request of Randolph Schuyler's was not to be thoughtlessly refused, so Steele acquiesced.

He was reticent in further dilating on Schuyler's character. Said he often called on ladies who could not be called exclusive, but denied knowledge of definite cases or names.

On the whole, Steele's evidence didn't get us anywhere. We already knew that Schuyler had gone to

Vicky Van's under an assumed name. The reason for this had little, if anything, to do with what had followed. A connection of some sort, between Vicky and Mr. Schuyler must be traced, in order to arrive at her possible motive. A woman does not stab to kill a chance guest whom she has never met before!

Bert Garrison came next. His talk ran mostly to eulogies of Vicky. The poor fellow was dead in love with her, and had been for many moons, but though Vicky favored him more than some others, yet she gave him no definite encouragement, as he himself ruefully admitted. But he made a desperate effort to show that a girl of Victoria Van Allen's high character and fine qualities would be incapable of a base deed.

The coroner smiled a little at Garrison's vehemence, and let him run on for a time, in praise of the absent Vicky.

At last, he said, "And, why, then, Mr. Garrison, in your opinion has Miss Van Allen disappeared?"

"The disappearance is not of her own volition," declared Garrison; "she has been taken away by somebody and held against her will, in order to make her appear guilty."

This was a new theory. I might have given it serious consideration had I not had speech with the girl herself. It couldn't be that Vicky was held captive, since she was at her own house two nights after the crime. But I could see that the jury, and even the coroner and detectives were interested in this idea.

"By whom could she possibly, or theoretically, he thus held?" the coroner asked.

"I don't know. But assuming some intruder effected an entrance and stabbed Mr. Schuyler, if surprised during or after the act by the sudden appearance of Miss Van Allen in the dining room, he might in some way have gotten her out of the house, and still be keeping her in a hiding-place."

It was perhaps, a possibility, but I didn't see how any intruder could do all that, without being seen by the waiters. Unless, perchance, the waiters had been bribed to silence. And that, in the face of Luigi's earnest, and convincing testimony, I could not believe.

It was a fantastic theory, evolved in the brain of Garrison, for the purpose of diverting suspicion from Vicky Van. However, it seemed to impress the coroner, and he made notes as he dismissed the witness.

Cassie Weldon added one bit of new information. She said, though with evident reluctance, that she had caught a mere glimpse of somebody running upstairs, just before the waiter had come to call for help.

Cassie had not wanted to testify at all. As she had intimated to me, it was detrimental to her work as a concert singer to be mixed up in this affair. But since she had to give her testimony, she apparently felt it her duty to tell the whole truth.

"How could you see the stairs from the living-room?" asked the interested coroner.

"I was near the door, and though I was not looking out into the hall, I had a vague, fleeting impression of somebody running upstairs. I paid no attention to it, of course, but I am sure somebody did."

"A man or a woman?"

"A woman. That is, I was conscious of a flutter of skirts, but I am not sure it was Miss Van Allen. I didn't see her clearly enough even to notice the color of her gown. It was merely a glimpse of some one flying round the newel post and up the stairs. It might have been a stranger."

"You mean, if there were some intruder, it may have been a woman, and not a man?"

"I don't know, I tell you. I can only say I know somebody ran upstairs. Further than that, I've no idea concerning it."

"It must have been Miss Van Allen," said the coroner, decidedly; "had it been any other woman, and had she stabbed Mr. Schuyler, Miss Van Allen would not have disappeared. Now, if this woman who ran upstairs was Miss Van Allen, she effected an escape from the upper stories. Is there a skylight exit?"

No one seemed to know, as no one had thought of Vicky Van leaving her house by such means.

But to me, the idea was ridiculous. A girl, in elaborate evening gown, clambering out of a skylight trap-door, to where? Not to a neighbor's, for Vicky Van knew none of the nearby residents. I had heard her say so, myself. And had she descended into a strange household, and begged for shelter, it would have become known before this.

Well, anyway, the detective Lowney immediately sent an order to have the skylight matter looked into and the proceedings went on.

Ariadne Gale was closely questioned as to how she knew of the picture in the back of Randolph Schuyler's watch. But she declared that he had shown it to her during their conversation that evening.

"I never saw the man before," said Ariadne, who unlike Cassie Weldon, rather enjoyed the publicity of the occasion. "I chanced to be about the first girl he was introduced to, when he came into the house. And we had a chat, and when I chaffed him a bit on his dignity and awe-inspiring presence, he refuted it by showing me the picture in his watch. He said it was a little chorus girl he had taken out to supper the night before. I could see the picture had been merely tucked in temporarily, it wasn't neatly pasted in, as a watch-case picture usually is, and then I chaffed him on his fickleness. Our conversation was the merest foolery, and a moment after, he went over to be presented to Miss Van Allen."

"You think they had never met before?"

"I'm sure they had not. They looked at each other with the conventional politeness of strangers, I know Miss Van Allen well, and she is not one to dissemble or pretend. I am sure she had never laid eyes on that man before. She simply couldn't have killed him!"

Ariadne's further evidence amounted to nothing, nor did that of several other of the party guests who were called on.

Except Mrs. Reeves. She knew more of Vicky's home life than any of the rest of us, but even she knew nothing of the girl's origin.

She had first met her at one of Miss Gale's studio parties, and had taken a fancy to her at once.

"Where did you first meet her, Miss Gale," the coroner interrupted to ask.

"She came to my studio to look at my pictures," was the reply. "She admired them, and bought one. She was so pleasant and so interested in my work that she came two or three times, and then I invited her to one of my little studio affairs. She quickly made friends, and she invited us to her house. I went there first about two years ago."

"So did I," Mrs. Reeves resumed. "And since then, I have been there frequently, and every time I saw the girl I liked her better. But she was always a bit of a mystery. I confess I tried at times, to learn something of her previous life. But she adroitly evaded my questions, and cleverly changed the subject. I think, however, from chance hints she let drop, that her home was somewhere in the Middle West."

"An indefinite term," observed Coroner Fenn.

"It's all I know."

"Where did Miss Van Allen go on her frequent absences from her home?"

"That I don't know, either. Often she'd be away a week, and on her return would tell of a gay house party down on Long Island or a week-end trip up Westchester way, but I don't remember any definite place she visited."

"I do," piped up Ariadne. "She often goes to Greenwich, Connecticut, and to Bronxville. I've heard her tell of these trips. She has a wide circle of acquaintances and, of course, she's a favorite with all who know her."

"I have a piece of evidence," resumed Mrs. Reeves, "which I daresay I ought to exhibit. It is a letter from Miss Van Allen, which I received only this morning."

This caused a sensation. A letter from Vicky Van! Just received! I found myself trembling in my shoes. And I asked myself why. Was I afraid the girl would be caught? Did I want to shield a felon? And I had to admit to myself that I did. I wasn't in love with Vicky Van, but I had a tremendous interest in her, and I didn't want that little lone, helpless person haled before a court of justice. Vicky did seem terribly alone. Hosts of friends she had, but no one who was in any way responsible for her, or in a position to help her. Well, if she ever returned, voluntarily or perforce, she would find a friend and champion in one Chester Calhoun, of that I was certain!

Mrs. Reeves handed her letter over to the coroner, and he read it out. It ran:

My dear Mrs. Reeves: You have always been such a good friend to me that I'm writing you just a line. You are everything that is good and kind, and now I'm going to ask you as a final favor to forget Vicky Van at once and forever. I am going away and I shall never return. Don't think of me any more hardly than you must, but if you can keep any loving little memory of the hours we spent together, I want you to do so. And as a remembrance, I want you to have my little electric coupe. It is in Rennard's garage, and I have written him to turn it over to you. I shall miss our happy times together, but—I can never come back. Do not worry about me, I am safe. And I am your affectionate Vicky Van.

"You are sure this is from Miss Van Allen?" asked Fenn.

"Oh, yes," replied Mrs. Reeves. "There's no mistaking that writing."

Nor was there. I knew Vicky's penmanship, and it was most peculiar. Never have I seen such a hand. Angular, slightly backhanded, and full of character, it would be difficult to imitate it, and, too, no one would have any reason to forge that letter to Mrs. Reeves. She had verified Vicky's statement, and found that a letter to the garage owner had instructed him to give up the car to Mrs. Reeves, and he had already done so, that very morning.

The letters had both been mailed in New York the night before, the postmark showing that they were mailed in the district that included Vicky's residence.

Was she, then, even now in hiding near her home? Or, had she sent the letters to be mailed by some one else? By Julie, perhaps, who, I felt sure, was with her mistress, wherever that might be.

My leaping thoughts took in all this, and by degrees the slower going coroner, put it in words.

Lowney, the detective, bristled with interest. A clue, he had, he thought, but what a clue! Two letters posted in the city. What did they show of the whereabouts of the missing girl?

Lowney scrutinized the one to Mrs. Reeves. Ordinary paper, such as might be bought in any stationery or department store, no monogram or initial on it, nor was there any maker's name under the flap.

But a dozen people present testified to Vicky's handwriting, and the coroner eagerly took possession of the letter.

Sherlock Holmes, I thought to myself, would read that letter, look at it through his good old lens, smell it, and then walk out, and return in a half hour, with Vicky Van in tow!

But for my part, I could see nothing illuminating in that plain paper and envelope, and the letter in the well-known penmanship.

All I gathered was, that wherever Vicky was, she was not only safe but comfortable. The tenor of the note breathed leisure and composure. Clearly, she was not

breathlessly hurrying from one place to another, or
vigilantly eluding pursuit. She was at ease, with
opportunity to indulge in thoughtful kindness to a friend,
and to write at length about herself.

At length, yes, but with no hint of her hiding-place
nor any clue to it. Poor little Vicky! She seemed so
alone—and yet—how did I know? She may have gone to
friends or—somehow I hated to think that she had any
man who was her legal—or even willing protector.

Yet she said she was safe, and her letter showed no
fear of the future. And then again I was stabbed by the
thought that perhaps there was no earthly future for
Vicky Van. I didn't want her to kill herself—I didn't want
her to be found and arrested—what did I want? I wasn't
sure in my own mind, save that I wanted her safety above
all else. I suppose I believed her guilty—I could believe
nothing else, but even so, I didn't want her brought to
bay.

I gave my own testimony, which was all true, and all
frank, except that I said nothing of my nocturnal visit to
Vicky's house or of our telephone conversation. If my
conscience smote me I combated it with my chivalry,
which would not allow me to betray a woman into the
hands of the law.

The later witnesses, who were mostly the working
people whom Vicky employed by the day, told nothing of
her or of her home life. They all spoke of her as a kind
lady to work for, though, as a rule, they had not seen her,
but had been engaged, directed and paid by the maid,
Julie.

It seemed to be tacitly assumed that wherever Vicky
was Julie was with her. I had had this information from
Vicky herself, but others took it for granted, in the
absence of any reason to think the contrary.

The whole day's session, to my mind, achieved little of
useful information. Mrs. Reeves' letter proved
conclusively that Vicky was aware of the search being
made for her, and showed her determination not to be

found. It was Saturday, and when the inquest was adjourned until Monday morning, I couldn't help feeling that it might as well have been permanently adjourned, for all the further conclusions it would lead to.

I went home at last, thrilling with the thought that that night I was to get Vicky's mail from her box and hide it where she had directed. I secretly hoped she might be in the house herself, waiting for it, but scarcely dared believe this would be the case.

CHAPTER 11: A NOTE FROM VICKY

Nor was it. I had secured a latch-key to the house, from the police, who were willing enough for me to search for possible clues, as I had told them I would do.

At their wits' end to locate Vicky Van, they welcomed my help and felt that as a friend of hers, I might learn more than a disinterested policeman could.

So, well after midnight, watching my chance when the patrolman had just passed on his regular round, I went across the street.

Easily I opened the mailbox and extracted a quantity of letters.

Quietly, then, I opened the house door and went in.

I had provided myself with a pocket flashlight, as I didn't want to illuminate the house, and I went at once to the music room, to perform my errand.

How strange it seemed! The lovely room, with dainty white and gold furnishings, reminded me so forcibly of the bewitching girl who owned it all. A thousand questions rose in my mind. What would become of that bijou residence? The bric-a-brac and pictures, the rugs and furniture, while not magnificent, were of the best, and many of them costly. The great Chinese vase, into which I was to drop the letters was a gem of its kind, though not anything a connoisseur would covet.

I raised the dragon-topped lid, and let the letters fall in. Replacing the lid, I still lingered. My errand was done, but I felt an impulse to stay. Everything spoke to me of Vicky Van. Where was she now? Making sure that the opaque blinds were drawn, I dared to turn on one tiny electric lamp. The faint light made the shadowed room lovelier than ever. Could a girl of such cultivated tastes and such refinement of character be a—a wrong-doer? I

couldn't say murderer even to myself. Then my common
sense flared up, and told me that crime is no respecter of
persons. That women who had slain human beings were
not necessarily of this or that walk of life. Granted a
woman had a motive to kill a man, that motive lay in the
impulses of her feminine nature, and revenge, jealousy,
fear, love or hate—whatever the motive, it was of deep
and over-powering and might find its root in equal
likeliness in the breast of queen or beggarmaid. I could
not say Vicky was incapable of crime—indeed, her gay,
volatile manner might hide a deeply perturbed spirit. She
was an enigma, and I—I must solve the riddle. I felt I
should never rest, until I knew the truth, and if Vicky
were a martyr to circumstances, or a victim to Fate, I
must know all about it.

Alone there, in the midnight hours, I resolved to
devote my time, all I could spare, my energies, all I could
command, and my life, so far as I might, to the discovery
of the truth, and I might or might not reveal my findings
as seemed to me best.

Leaving the music room, I went back through the long
hall, and passed the door of Vicky's bedroom. Reverently I
looked inside. The very walls seemed crying for her to
come back. Would she ever so do? I wandered on through
the bedroom, and even looked in the dressing room. I felt
no compunction. It was not from idle curiosity, rather, I
walked as one at a shrine. The exquisitely feminine
boudoir was a mute witness to a love of beauty and art. I
used only my flashlight, but on an impulse, I turned on
one light by the side of the long mirror. I looked in it, as
Vicky must often have done when dressing for her
parties, as, indeed, she must have done, when dressing
that last fatal night and seeing my own grim reflection, I
gravely nodded my head at myself, and whispered, "We'll
find the truth, old man, you see if we don't!"

In the ornate Florentine frame, with its branching
arabesques, was a strand of the gold beads that had
adorned Vicky's gown that night. I visualized her,

whirling her skirts about before the mirror, with that quick, lithe grace of hers, and catching the fluttering fringe in the gilt protuberance. Perhaps she exclaimed in petulance, but, more likely, I thought, she laughed at the trivial accident. That was Vicky Van, as I knew her, to laugh at a mischance, and smile good-naturedly at an accident.

I lifted the strand of little beads from the entangling frame, and put it away in my pocketbook, as a dear and intimate souvenir of the girl I had known. Then, with a final glance that was a sort of farewell, I glimpsed the pretty, cosy nest, and went downstairs.

Here I paused again. Cassie Weldon had said she could see the staircase from the door of the living-room. I tried it. She was right. A person standing just inside the living-room door, could catch sight of a person on the stairs. And, as Cassie, said, she was not looking that way, but was partly conscious of some one running up the stairs. It might well be. She would naturally give the incident no thought at the moment—it was strange she had even remembered it. And it may have been Vicky. Then she might have descended by the rear staircase, there probably was one, I didn't know. And anyway, what mattered it how she had left the house? She had left it, and had not returned.

I remembered the allusion to the skylight. In a jiffy, I had run upstairs clear to the highest story. There was a skylight, or scuttle, rather, and it was bolted on the inside.

That settled that. Vicky Van had not climbed out that way, and I for one, never supposed she had.

Strangely reluctant to leave the house, I went downstairs again, looked into the living-room, and passed on to the dining-room. I contemplated the sideboard, in front of which Randolph Schuyler had met his death. Many pieces of silver and glass stood upon it, and all was in order, as if it had been carefully looked after for the party occasion.

Without consciously noting details, I chanced to observe that a small silver-handled carving fork, was lacking its knife. I had no knowledge of Vicky Van's table appurtenances, but the way the fork lay looked to me as if the knife had lain across it, and had been removed.

I had no concern over it, for I knew the knife that had stabbed Schuyler was now in possession of the police, and this one had doubtless been used in preparation of the supper, if indeed, there was a knife belonging to the fork.

It was a matter of no moment, but somehow it stuck in my mind. If Vicky or rather, if Julie had straightened up things on the sideboard in the process of tidying up for the party, would she not have laid the fork a different way, unless there had been a matching knife to lay across it? I suppose the whole question came into my mind, because at home, we had a beefsteak carving set that always lay crossed on the sideboard. A man gets accustomed to the sight of such household details, and they photographed on his memory.

Well, anyway, I looked for that knife. I even went to the butler's pantry and looked, but I didn't see it. The pantry had been hastily evacuated by the caterer's men, and though tidied, it was not in spick and span condition. You see, having lived so long with two such homey bodies as Aunt Lucy and Win, I was not utterly unversed in domestic matters. The pantry was well equipped with modern utensils and implements, and all its appointments spoke of the taste and efficiency of its mistress.

"Poor Vicky," I sighed to myself," poor, dear little Vicky Van!" and then I went softly out of the front door and down the steps

I went slowly, and looked back several times, in a vague hope that Vicky might emerge from some nearby shadow and go into the house for her letters. But I saw no sign of such a happening, and went on home, my heart full of a gloomy foreboding that I would never see her again.

"Going to work on Sunday, Winnie?" I asked, as next morning, my sister appeared, garbed for the street.

"Not regularly to work, but Mrs. Schuyler wants me to look after some matters of confidence."

"Oho, how important we are!" I chaffed her. "When does the Crowell lady come into her own?"

"Not for another week. She isn't quite ready to come, and Mrs. Schuyler is willing to keep me on a while longer."

"I don't blame her," and I looked at my pretty, bright-faced sister with approval. "I say, old girl, s'pose I stroll over with you."

"Come along. Though I'm not sure Mrs. Schuyler will see you. She usually sends me to receive callers."

"Well, Little Miss Manage-It, I could even live through that. And perhaps I'll get a look-in with the fair sisters-in-law."

"That, surely, if you wish. They're ready and eager to see visitors. I believe they love to go over the details of the whole affair with anyone who will listen."

"Oh, come now, Win, not as bad as that."

"They don't think it's bad. They're bound to track down the Van Allen girl, and they hold the opinion that everybody they get hold of may be an important witness. They go over the reports from the inquest all the time, and can hardly wait till tomorrow to see what will come out next."

"Me for them," I responded. "I'd like a good chat on the subject."

We went over to the Fifth Avenue house, and were admitted by the solemn and wise-eyed butler. I was shown to the library, while Winnie was directed to go to Mrs. Schuyler's room.

But it was not long before we were all together in the library—widow, sisters, and all, for Lowney had made a discovery and he proposed to tell the family of it.

Win and I were allowed to be present, and the detective showed his new find.

It seems he had been searching the papers and letters of the late Mr. Schuyler. This had been not only permitted by the wife, but had been urged by the sisters, who hoped it might result in some further light on the mysterious Miss Van Allen. And it did. In the desk, in a secret compartment—which was not so secret but that the detective could open it—were a number of letters from feminine pens, and a number of receipted bills for jeweled trinkets, presumably sent to these or other ladies, for they were not of a sort affected by Ruth Schuyler or the two sisters. A blue enameled watch bracelet, and a rhinestone tiara were representative purchases entered on these bills.

But the pile of letters sank into insignificance, when we learned the fact that there was a letter from Vicky Van among them!

Regardless of Mrs. Schuyler's feelings, Lowney read the letter aloud. This was it:

My Dear Mr. Schuyler: I enjoyed your supper party, and it was good of you to give me inside information about the stocks. But I must beg of you to cease your further attentions to me, as I cannot number on my list of calling acquaintances the husband of another woman. I am, perhaps, rather prudish in my view of life, but this is one of my inviolable rules. Very truly yours, Victoria Van Allen.

I knew that before. Vicky Van, living alone and unchaperoned, save for the ubiquitous Julie, flouted convention in many ways, but it was as she said, her inviolable rule to receive no married man without his wife at her parties. Nor was there often occasion for her to use this stipulation. The young people whom I had met at her house, had always been maids and bachelors, and now and then, a young married couple who playfully enacted a chaperon part. Mrs. Reeves, a widow, was probably the oldest of the crowd, but she was well under forty.

It was quite true, no married man, and indeed, no man of the type or age of Randolph Schuyler, had ever, to my knowledge, enjoyed the friendship of Vicky Van. But not for a minute, did I think that she would go so far as to kill him for daring to enter her house! That was unthinkable.

And yet, it seemed so to Lowney, and, apparently, to the sisters of the dead man.

She declared that the letter proved that Randolph had intruded on her acquaintance, and she had objected from coyness or coquetry; and that when he persisted, she was so enraged that she flew into a passion and wilfully ended his life.

"I can't think that," said Ruth Schuyler, wearily. "It seems more to me as if that letter exculpates the girl. She was quite evidently not in love with my husband, and she honestly tried to make him understand her scruples. So I can't think she killed him. I did think so at first, of course, but on thinking things over, and in the light of this letter, I begin to believe her innocent. What date does the letter bear?"

"There's no date," said Lowney, looking at the paper. "It was not in an envelope—"

"Then how did it reach my husband?"

"Oh, of course, it came in an envelope, I suppose, but I found none with it. So we can't tell where it was sent, here or to one of his clubs or to his office address."

"Not here, I'm sure," said Mrs. Schuyler. "Probably to his club. You are quite welcome to the letter, Mr. Lowney. Make what use you think best of it. If it serves to establish Miss Van Allen's innocence, I shall be rather glad. But if it seems to throw further suspicion on her, then justice must be done."

"Of course, it throws suspicion on that woman!" declared Miss Rhoda Schuyler, with a vindictive glance at the letter in Lowney's hand. "The hussy, to write to Randolph at all!"

"But," I interposed, unable to stand this unjust speech, "Mr. Schuyler must have made advances to her first."

"She lured him on. I've heard you say yourself, Mr. Calhoun, that this Van Allen person is a siren, a—"

"Now, now, Miss Rhoda," I began, but the other sister chimed in.

"Of course she is! Of course, the wrong was mostly hers. And she killed Randolph, I know it! Why, the waiter man saw her! Go ahead, Mr. Lowney, hunt her down, and bring her to account. I never shall sleep peacefully until my brother's death is avenged! I cannot understand, Ruth, how you can be so indifferent."

A flush rose to Ruth Schuyler's cheek, and, enlightened anew to her husband's character by that letter, I began to feel a different sort of sympathy for the widow.

Randolph Schuyler had been unfaithful, he had been domineering and tyrannical, and I knew he had not allowed his wife to have the comforts and luxuries she desired, although he was enormously wealthy.

A social secretary, for instance. Most women of Ruth Schuyler's rank in society had that necessary assistant, yet, during Schuyler's life his wife was forbidden the favor.

Winnie had told me this, and had told me much more, that proved how unjust and unkind Randolph Schuyler had been. The sisters, too, shared his views, and as a consequence, the household was run on old-fashioned lines that ill accord with the ways of to-day.

Mrs. Schuyler had in no way complained, Win told me, but it was easily seen how matters stood. It fell to Winnie's lot to order many things from the shops— stationery, mourning apparel, and house needs. These, my sister said, were ordered with the most perfect taste, but with a lavishness, which was indubitably unusual to Ruth Schuyler.

The sisters exclaimed at the extravagance, but Ruth, though listening politely, serenely went her own way, and carried out her own plans. In the matter of fresh flowers, she was like a child, Win said, and she enjoyed the blossoms she ordered as if she had hungered for them for years. Winnie was growing deeply attached to her employer, if that word is applicable, and Ruth Schuyler was fond of Win.

But I am digressing. Mrs. Schuyler replied to her sister-in-law's speech by saying, gently, "I am not indifferent, Sarah, but it seems to me we have no real evidence against the girl, and—"

"No real evidence! When she was caught red-handed! Or nearly caught! If that stupid waiter had had sense enough to jump and grab her, we would have had no search to make at all!"

"It may be so, Sarah, you may be right. But until you do find her don't condemn her utterly. From what Mr. Calhoun has told me of her and from the tone of that letter she wrote to Randolph, I can't make it seem possible that she killed a man she knew so slightly. And yet, it may be she did."

"Well," remarked Lowney, "the note proves that she had seen Mr. Schuyler before, anyway. Then, when he came to her house as Mr. Somers, she was naturally annoyed, as she had asked him not to do so. And all that is against the girl, I say. But it remains to be seen what the coroner's jury will think of it."

"They'll see it in its true light," declared Rhoda Schuyler. "Of course, she was angry when he came to her house after being forbidden, unless the sly thing wrote the note just to lure him on, but in any case, she was alone with him, she used the knife on him and she ran away. What more evidence do you need? Now, to find her.

That's a task I shall never give up or neglect until I've accomplished it."

"And you are right, Rhoda," said Ruth, "if the girl is guilty. I hope she will be found, for I'm sure the truth could then be learned, whether she is guilty or not."

"Will you come, now, Mrs. Schuyler," said Tibbetts, from the doorway. "The flowers have arrived."

Ruth, beckoning to Winnie, rose, and the two left the room.

"Perfectly idiotic," said Sarah, "the way she orders flowers! Fresh ones every day!"

"But hasn't she a right to spend her own money as she likes?" I defended.

"A legal right, perhaps," was the retort, "but not a moral right to disregard her husband's wishes so utterly"

CHAPTER 12: MORE NOTES

Next morning at breakfast, there was but one topic of conversation. Indeed, little else had been talked of for days but the Schuyler case and all its side issues.

Winnie held forth at length on the martyrdom Ruth Schuyler had suffered because of the cruelty of her late husband.

"He wasn't really ugly, you know," explained Win, "and I don't say she's glad he's dead. But he thwarted her in every little way that she wanted to enjoy herself. They had a box at the opera, and a big country house and all that, but he wouldn't let her go to matinees or have a motor of her own or buy anything until he had passed judgment on it. She even had to submit her costume designs to him, and if he approved the dressmaker made them up. And he wouldn't let her have fashionable clothes. They had to be plain and of rich heavy materials, such as the sisters wear. Mr. Schuyler was under the thumb of those two old maids, and Rhoda, especially, put him up to all sorts of schemes to bother Ruth."

"Do you call her Ruth?" I asked, in surprise.

"Yes, she told me I might. She's lovely to me, and I'm so glad to do all I can for her. Honest, Chet, she lived an awful life with that man."

"I'd like to see her," said Aunt Lucy." All you've said about her, Winnie, makes me a bit curious."

"So you shall, Auntie, some time. She's a real friend of mine now, and even after Edith Crowell goes there as secretary, she says I must often go to see her as her friend."

"She's charming," I declared. "Every time I see her I'm more impressed with her gentle dignity. And I don't know how she can be so decent to those two old women."

"Nor I," agreed Win, as Aunt Lucy asked, "Is she pretty?"

"Is she, Winnie?" I said.

"Well, she is and she isn't. She's so colorless, you know. Her hair is that flat ashy blonde, and she's so pale always. Then her eyes and lashes are so light, and—well, ineffective. But her expression is so sweet, and when once in a while she laughs outright, she's very attractive. And she's such a thoroughbred. She never errs in taste or judgment. She knows just what to reply to all the queer letters of condolence that come to her, and just how to talk to the people who call. And that's another thing. She hasn't any friends of her own age. She knows only the people who belong to the most exclusive set, and they're nearly all the age of the old sisters. But Mrs. Schuyler is lovely to them. And in her soft pretty black gowns she looks a whole lot better than she ever did in the ones she wore while he was alive. I've seen them in her wardrobe, and I've seen her try on some that she was going to give away, and they're sights! Elegant, you know, but not the thing for her. Now, that she can select her own, she has beauties."

"She certainly must be glad, then, to be freed from such a tyrant," said Aunt Lucy.

"Now don't you think that!" insisted Winnie, earnestly. "She may feel, so, 'way down in her deepest heart, but she won't admit it, even to herself. And, of course, no matter how much she didn't love him, she wouldn't want him taken off that way! No, she's perfectly all right, and she mourns that man just as sincerely as any woman could mourn a man who didn't understand her."

I looked at Win in amazement. Little sister was growing up, it seemed. Well, the experience would do her no harm. Ruth Schuyler's influence could work only for good, and a taste of real life would give a wider outlook than Win could get at home.

I went down to the coroner's courtroom. The inquest was proceeding in its usual discursive way, and I sat down to listen for a while. The coroner was hearing reports from detectives who had interviewed the market men and shopkeepers where Vicky Van had bought wares.

It was just what might be expected from any householder's record. Vicky had always paid her bills promptly, usually by check on a well-known bank. Sometimes, if the bills were small they were paid in cash. In such case Miss Van Allen herself or the maid brought the money; if checks, they were sent by mail. The garage man reported a similar state of affairs. His monthly bills were promptly paid, and Miss Van Allen had found no fault with his service. She was away from home frequently, but when at home, she used her motor car often and was kind to the chauffeur who drove her. This chauffeur told of taking her to the shops, to the theatre, to friends' houses and to picture galleries—but had never been directed to any place where a lady might not go.

The bank people said that Miss Van Allen had had an account with them for years, but as their depositors were entitled to confidential dealings they would say little more. They stated, however, that Miss Van Allen was a most desirable patron and never overdrew her account or made trouble of any sort.

There was nothing to be gleaned from this kind of testimony. We all knew that Vicky was a good citizen and all this was merely corroboration. What was wanted was some hint of her present whereabouts.

Lowney had tried to get at this by the use of an address book he had found in Vicky Van's desk. He had telephoned or called on many of the people whose addresses were in the book, but all said over and over what we already knew.

Personally, I felt sure that Vicky was staying with some friend not far from her own house. It could well be, that somebody cared enough for the girl to hide her from the authorities. This, however, argued her guilty, for otherwise, a true friend would persuade her that the wiser course would be to disclose herself to the public.

However, nothing transpired to bear out my opinion, and as the list of witnesses dwindled, no progress was made toward a solution of the mystery. And so, when at last, an open verdict was returned, with no mention of Vicky's name, I was decidedly relieved, but I didn't see how it could have been otherwise.

I dropped in at the Schuyler house on my way home. I was beginning to feel on a very friendly footing there, and, partly owing to Winnie's graphic powers of narration, I took an increasing interest in Ruth Schuyler.

As Win had said, she looked charming, although pathetic in her black robes. She permitted herself a touch of white at the turned-in throat, and a white flower was tucked in her bodice. A contrast, indeed, to the severe garb of the spinster sisters, who looked like allegorical figures of hopeless gloom.

But their manner was more of militant revenge, and, having heard the verdict of the coroner's jury, they were ready to take up the case themselves.

"Come in, Mr. Calhoun," they called out, as I entered the library, "you're just the man we want to see. Now, that the coroner has finished his task, we will take the matter up. Mr. Lowney, I suppose, will continue the search for Miss Van Allen, but we fear he will not be successful. So, we have determined to send for the great detective, Fleming Stone."

"Stone!" I cried, "why, he won't work with the police."

"Then he can work without them," declared Rhoda, with asperity. "I've heard wonderful stories of that man's success, and we're going to engage him at once."

"He's very expensive," I began.

"No matter. We're going to find our brother's murderer if it takes every penny of our fortune."

"What do you think of this plan, Mrs. Schuyler?" I asked.

"I've not been consulted" she said, with a slight smile. "Since Mr. Randolph's sisters choose to adopt it, I have no reason to object. I know nothing of Mr. Stone, but if he is really a great detective, he will not condemn that girl unheard. And if she is proved guilty, of course the claims of justice must be met. Do you know him, Mr. Calhoun?"

"Not personally. I've often heard of him, and he's a wonder. If you want to find Miss Van Allen, you can't do better than to get him on the trail. If he can't find her, nobody can."

"That's what I say," put in Sarah. "And if he doesn't find her, at least we've the satisfaction of knowing we've done all we could."

"We thought of offering a reward for information of Miss Van Allen," added Rhoda, "but if we're going to get Mr. Stone, wouldn't it be better to consult him about that?"

"I think it would," I judged.

Just then Winnie came into the room. She had been writing notes, and she held a lot of unopened letters in her hand.

"Oh, Ruth," she cried, "what do you think! Here's the mail, Jepson just gave it to me, and there's a letter for you from Miss Van Allen!"

"What!" cried everybody at once.

"Yes," declared Winnie, "I know the hand, it's the same as was on that letter to Mr. Schuyler. It's such a queer hand, you can't forget it."

She handed all the letters to Ruth, the one she referred to on top.

Mrs. Schuyler turned pale as she looked at the envelope. I glanced at it, too, and without doubt, it was Vicky Van's writing.

It had been mailed in New York that same morning, and delivered just now, about five o'clock.

"You open it, Mr. Calhoun," said Ruth, as if she shrank from the task.

I took it gravely, for it seemed to me to portend trouble for little Vicky. Was she giving herself up, or what?

Win handed me a letter-opener, and I slit the envelope.

As they breathlessly awaited my words, I read:

To Mrs. Randolph Schuyler: Dear Madam: It is useless to look for me. To-day I am leaving New York forever. The mystery of Mr. Schuyler's death will never be solved, the truth never learned. I alone know the secret and it will die with me. You may employ detectives from now till doomsday but you will discover nothing. So give up the search, for you will never find Victoria Van Allen.

There was a pause as I finished reading. Myself, I was thrilled by a certain phrase in the letter. Vicky said, "the secret will die with me." Again, I felt that she was intending to bring about her own death, and that speedily. Would we know it if she did? I was thinking deeply, when Miss Rhoda, spoke:

"I believe that girl means to kill herself, and I should think she would!"

"Why do you think that?" and Ruth looked up with a startled face.

"It sounds so, and it would be the natural outcome of her remorse at her dreadful deed."

"I think she must be guilty," said Winnie, her dear little countenance drawn with grief, as she studied the letter for herself.

None of us said much more. We all were stunned in a way, by this unexpected development, and had to readjust our theories.

"Well," Miss Rhoda said, decidedly, "I shall consult Mr. Stone, anyway. I've written him, and though I've not mailed the letter yet, I shall send it off to-night. Then when he comes to talk it over we can see what he says and abide by his judgment."

"That's a good idea, Rhoda," and Ruth Schuyler nodded assentingly; "I, too, want justice, and if Fleming Stone thinks he can find Miss Van Allen, let him do so."

It was six o'clock then, and Win and I went home, leaving the Schuyler ladies to their own discussions.

Ruth Schuyler's hand lingered a moment in mine, as I bade her adieu, and she said, wistfully, "I wish you would tell me just what you think we had better do. I am so unaccustomed to judging for myself in any important matter."

"I think it is wise to get Mr. Stone," I returned. "In any case it can do no harm, you know."

"No, I suppose not," and she gave me one of her rare smiles of appreciation. "I am glad you are looking after us, instead of Mr. Bradbury," she said further, and I sincerely responded that I was glad, too.

Another surprise awaited me at home. On the hall table lay my own mail, and as I picked it up, and ran the letters over, there was one from Vicky Van.

I hastily concealed it from Winnie's sharp eyes, for I had no notion what it might divulge, and hurried with it up to my own room.

Impatiently I tore it open and raced through its contents.

Dear Mr. Calhoun: Thank you deeply for attending to my errand. Owing to your kindness I received the letters I wanted. Now, will you do me one last favor? Come again to the house tonight, and take a small parcel which you will find in the Chinese jar in the music room. Keep this for me and if I do not ask you for it within a year, destroy it unopened. I wish I could be more frank with you, you have proved yourself such a staunch friend, but I cannot control circumstances and so I must bear my fate. I do not know what Mrs. Schuyler will think of it, but I have written her a letter. When you see her, try to make her realize it is useless to hunt for me. Since I can keep hidden for this length of time, my retreat is not likely to be discovered. And now, my kindest of friends, good-bye. Vicky Van.

I stood, staring at the letter. I read it through a dozen times. Of course, I would do her bidding, but my heart rebelled at the finality of the lines. I knew I would never hear from Vicky Van again. As she said, since we hadn't traced her yet, we never could.

I wondered where she could possibly be. And Julie, too. Somebody was shielding them both. They couldn't be disguised or anything of that sort, for they had left the house at dead of night, without luggage or—and I hadn't thought of this before—without money! How could they have found shelter, save in some friend's house?

Of course, Vicky could have snatched up a purse as she ran. Perhaps that was what she flew upstairs for. And then, maybe, she went down the back stairs—but no, the waiters must have seen her that way. And Luigi was in the front hall a moment after Vicky disappeared.

Aside from my personal interest, I hated to think I should never know just how she did get away. For now, I had no hope that Fleming Stone or anyone else could ever find the girl. She was too canny to be taken, after her successful concealment so far.

I went downstairs after a time, but I said nothing of my letter to Aunt Lucy or Win.

They were eagerly discussing the latest news, and Aunt Lucy was saying, "Yes, I've heard of Mr. Stone, and they do say he's a marvel. I hope he'll find the girl, if only to learn the mystery of her disappearance."

"Oh, he'll find her," assured Winnie, "I've heard a lot about him over there and he's a wizard! But I think he'll have a long chase."

"Meantime, what becomes of the house?" queried Aunt Lucy. "What does, Chet? Can anyone go in it who likes?"

"No," I returned, a little shortly, for I foresaw Aunt Lucy had that absurd feminine desire to pry into another person's home. "It's in charge of the police, and they won't let anyone in, without some very good reason."

"Couldn't you get in?"

"I suppose I might" I admitted unwillingly, "if I had any business there."

"Oh, do get up some business, Chet," begged Winnie, "and get the keys and let Auntie and me go with you! Oh, do! I'd love to see that girl's things!"

"Winnie, you're positively lowbred to show such curiosity!" I exclaimed, angrily—the more so, that I had the house key in my pocket at that moment. But I was glad I had not told them of Vicky Van's letter to me!

I waited until well past midnight, and then, after seeing the post patrol pass Vicky's door, I softly went out of my own house, and across the street.

I walked calmly up the steps of Vicky's home, and sadly put the latchkey in the door—for the last time. I felt as if I were performing funeral rites, and I entered and closed the door behind me, softly, as one does in the house of death.

I went up the stairs, in the gloom. It was not black darkness, for a partly raised blind gave me a glimmer of light from the street. Into the music room I went, and by my pocket flashlight, I took the lid from the Chinese jar. But there was no parcel inside!

Amazed, I threw the light down into the big vase, but it was utterly empty.

There was no use looking elsewhere for the parcel—I knew Vicky well enough to know that she would do exactly as she had said. Or, since she hadn't, I was sure that she would not have left that parcel in any other hiding-place.

I put the flashlight back in my pocket, and started downstairs.

Slowly I descended, for I still felt a little uncertain what to do. Should I wait for a short time, or go back home and return again later?

I reached the foot of the stairs, and concluded to go home, and then think out my next step.

As I passed the living-room door, I heard a low voice whisper my name.

I turned sharply. In the doorway, I could dimly discern a cloaked figure. "Hush!" she said, softly, and beckoned to me.

It was Vicky Van!

CHAPTER 13: FLEMING STONE

Vicky had said "Hush!" but it was an unnecessary precaution, for I was too stunned to articulate. I peered at her in the darkness and then, unable to control my desire for certainty I flashed my little pocket light on her for an instant.

"Don't!" she whispered, putting her hands up before her face.

But I had seen. It was really Vicky Van, her smooth black hair looped over her ears, her scarlet mouth, and soft pink cheeks, flushed with excitement of the moment, and her long dark lashes, which suddenly fell beneath the blinding flare of the light, all were those of the runaway girl.

"Don't talk," she said, hastily, "let me do the talking. I want you to help me, will you?"

"Of course, I will," and all sense of law and justice fled before the wave of pity and solicitude for the trembling suppliant who thus appealed to me.

Her voice was indistinct and a little hoarse, as if she was laboring under great mental and nerve strain, and she was so alone, so unprotected, that I couldn't help promising any assistance in my power.

"There wasn't any parcel in the big vase," I said, in a low voice, as she seemed to hesitate about going on with her explanation.

"No, here it is," and she handed me a little box, "Just put it away safely for the present. And now, this is what I want to ask of you. Don't let them engage that Mr. Stone, to hunt me down, will you?"

"Why, how can I help it?"

"Oh, can't you?" and she sounded so disappointed; "I hoped you could persuade Mrs. Schuyler not to have him."

"But Mrs. Schuyler doesn't want him, either!" I exclaimed. "It's those two sisters who insist on getting him. And I never could turn their wills, try as I might."

"Why doesn't Mrs. Schuyler want him?"

"Oh, I'm not sure that she really objects to the plan, but, I mean she didn't seem as anxious as the other two. You see, little girl, the widow of Randolph Schuyler isn't so bitter against you as the two sisters are."

"That's good of her," and Vicky's voice was wistful. "But, you know I must remain in hiding—"

"I thought you were going to leave New York?"

"I am. And at once. But if that Mr. Stone gets on my trail, he'll find me, as sure as fate. And so I risked this interview to try to persuade you to use your influence against his coming."

"And I'll do that," I returned, heartily. "But I feel that I ought to tell you that I doubt my power to dissuade the Schuyler sisters from their determination. And, too, how did you know they thought of getting him?"

"Oh, I see all the papers, you know, and in one of them a reporter gave a personal interview with the Schuyler people, and they hinted at getting that man."

Vicky sighed wearily, as if her last hope was gone. I was full of questions I wanted to ask her, but it seemed intrusive and unkind to quiz her. And yet, one thing I felt I must say. I must ask her what she knew of the actual crime.

"Tell me," I blurted out, "who did kill Randolph Schuyler?"

Again I felt her tremble, and her voice quivered as she whispered back, "It must have been some enemy of his, who got in at the window, or something like that."

My heart fell. This was the sort of thing she would say if she were herself the guilty one. I had hoped for a more sincere, even if despairing, answer.

"But I must send you away," she breathed in my ear. We were standing just inside the room, and Vicky held her hand on a chair-back for support. There was the faintest light from the street, enough for us to distinguish one another's forms, but no more. Vicky wore a street gown of some sort, and a long cloak. On her head was a small hat, and a black net veil. This was tied so tightly that it interfered a little with her speech, I thought, though when I had looked at her face by my flashlight, the veil had not been of sufficient thickness to conceal her features at all. I've often wondered why women wear those uncomfortable things. She kept pulling it away from her lips as she talked.

"I want my address book," she went on, hurriedly. "I've looked all over for it, and it's gone. Did the detective take it?"

"I think he did," I replied, remembering Lowney's search.

"Can't you get it back for me?"

"Look here, child, what do you think I am? A magician?"

"No, but I thought you could manage somehow to get it," her voice showed the adorable petulance that distinguished Vicky Van; "and then, you could send it to me—"

"Where?" I cried, eagerly. "Where shall I address you?"

"I can't tell you that. But you can bring it here and leave it in the Chinese jar, and I will get it."

"How do you come in and go out of this house without being seen?" I demanded. "By the area door?"

"Perhaps so," and she spoke lightly. "And perhaps by a window, and maybe by means of an aeroplane and down through the skylight."

"Not that," I said, "the skylight is fastened on the inside, and has been ever since—ever since that night."

"Well, then I don't come that way. But if you'll get that book and put it in the big vase, I'll come and get it. When will it be there?"

"You're crazy to think I can get it," I returned, slowly, "but if I can I will. Give me a few days—"

"A week, if you like. Shall we say a week from tonight?"

"Next Monday? Yes. If I can get it at all, I can have it by then. How shall I let you know?"

"You needn't let me know, for I know now you will get it. Steal it from Mr. Lowney, if you can't get it otherwise."

"But if Fleming Stone is on your trail, will you come for the book?"

"I must," she spoke gravely. "I must have the book. It means everything to me. I must have it!"

"Then you shall, if I can manage it. It is your book, it has proved of no value as evidence, you may as well have it."

"Yes, I may as well have it. And now, Mr. Calhoun, will you go, please, or do you intend to turn me over to the police?"

"Vicky!" I cried, "how can you say such a thing? Of course I'll go, if you bid me. But let me wait a minute. You know you wrote to Ruth Schuyler—"

"Ruth? Is that one of the old sisters?"

"No. Ruth is the widow."

"Oh, yes, I wrote to her. I didn't know her first name. I wrote because I thought it was she who is making the desperate search for me, and I hoped I could influence her to stop it. That's all. I have no interest in Randolph Schuyler's widow, except as she affects my future, but can you do anything by working in the other direction? I mean can you dissuade Fleming Stone from coming, by asking him not to? You can bribe him perhaps—I have money—"

"Oh, I doubt if I could do anything like that. But I'll try, I'll try every way I can, and, if I succeed—how shall I let you know?"

"Oh, I'll know. If he takes up the matter, it will probably get into the papers, and if I see nothing of it, I'll conclude you succeeded."

"But I—I want to see you again, Vicky—"

"Oh, no, you don't. Why, you don't know this minute but what I stabbed that man, and—"

"You didn't, Vicky—tell me you didn't!"

"I can't tell you that. I can't tell you anything. I am the most miserable girl on God's earth!" and I heard tears in Vicky's voice, and a sob choked her utterance.

"Now go," she said, after a moment, "I can't stand any more. Please go, and do what you can for me, without getting yourself into trouble. Go, and don't look back to see how I make my exit, will you?"

"Indeed, I won't do that. Your confidences are safe with me, Vicky, and I will do all in my power to help you, in any way I can."

"Then go now," she said, and a gentle pressure of her hand on my arm urged me toward the door.

I went without another word, and neither while in the street, nor after gaining my own house, did I look back for another glimpse of Vicky Van.

And yet, try as I would, maneuver as I might, I couldn't prevent the arrival of Fleming Stone.

The Schuyler sisters were determined to have the great detective, and though Mrs. Schuyler wasn't so anxious, yet she raised not the slightest objection, and after some persuasion, Stone agreed to take the case.

I was present at his first call to discuss details and was immensely interested in my first sight of the man.

Tall, well-formed, and of a gravely courteous manner, he impressed me as the most magnetically attractive man I had ever seen. His iron-gray hair and deep-set, dark eyes gave him a dignity that I had never before associated with my notions of a detective.

The Schuyler sisters were frankly delighted with him.

"I know you'll run down the murderer of my brother," Miss Rhoda exulted, while Miss Sarah began to babble volubly of what she called clues and evidence.

Fleming Stone listened politely, now and then asking a direct question and sometimes turning to Ruth Schuyler for further information.

As I watched him closely, it occurred to me that he really paid little attention to what the women said, he was more engaged in scanning their faces and noting their attitudes. Perhaps I imagined it, but I thought he was sizing up their characters and their sympathies, and intended looking up his clues and evidence by himself.

"The first thing to do," he declared, at last, "is to find Miss Van Allen."

This was what I had feared, and remembering my promise to Vicky I said, "I think that will be impossible, Mr. Stone. She wrote she was leaving New York forever."

"But a householder like that can't go away forever," Stone said, "she must look after her goods and chattels, and she must pay her rent—"

"No, she owns the house."

"Must pay the taxes, then. Must sell it, or rent it or do something with it."

"It would seem so," I agreed. "And yet, if one is wanted for murder one would sacrifice household goods and the house itself in order to escape being caught."

"True," and Stone nodded his head. "But, still, I fancy she would return for something. Few women could leave their home like that, and not have some valuables or some secret papers or something for which they must return. I venture to say Miss Van Allen has already been back to her house, more than once, on secret errands."

Was the man a clairvoyant? How could he know that Vicky had done this very thing? But I realized at once, that he knew it, not from cognizance of facts, but from his prescience of what would necessarily follow in such a case.

"She has her keys, of course?" he asked.

"The police have charge of the keys," I said, a little lamely.

"I know," Stone said, impatiently, "but there are doubtless more keys than the ones they have. I should say, that Miss Van Allen took at least the key of one door with her, however hurried her flight."

"It may be so," I conceded. "But, granting she has been back and forth on the errands you suggest, it is not likely she will keep it up."

"No, it is not. And especially if she learns I am on the case."

"How could she know that?" Ruth Schuyler asked.

"I'm sure Miss Van Allen is a most clever and ingenious young woman," Stone replied, "and I feel sure she knows all that is going on. She gets information from the papers, and, too, she has that dependable maid, Julie. That woman, probably disguised, can do much in the way of getting information as to how matters are progressing. You see, I've followed the case all the way along, and the peculiarities and unique conditions of it are what induced me to take it up."

"Shall we offer a reward, Mr. Stone, for the discovery of the hiding place of Miss Van Allen?" asked Rhoda, eagerly. "I want to use every possible means of finding her."

"Not yet, Miss Schuyler. Let us try other plans first. But I must enjoin utter secrecy about my connection with the matter. Not the fact that I am at work on it, but the developments or details of my work. It is a most unusual, a most peculiar case, and I must work unimpeded by outside advice or interference. I may say, I've never known of a case which presented such extraordinary features, and features which will either greatly simplify or greatly impede my progress."

"Just what do you mean by that last remark, Mr. Stone?" asked Ruth Schuyler, who had been listening intently.

"I mean that the absolutely mysterious disappearance of the young woman will either be of easy and simple solution, or else it will prove an insoluble mystery. There will be no half-way work about it. If I can't learn the truth in a short time, I fear I never can."

"How strange," said I. "Do you often feel thus about the beginning of a case?"

"Very rarely, almost never. And never have I felt it so strongly as in this instance. To trace that girl is not a matter of long and patient search, it's rather a question of a bit of luck or a slight slip on her part, or—well—of some coincidence or chance discovery that will clear things at one flash."

"Then you're depending on luck?" exclaimed Rhoda, in a disappointed tone.

"Oh, not that," and Stone smiled. "At least, I'm not depending entirely on that. If luck comes my way, so much the better. And now, please let me see the notes Miss Van Allen has written."

None was available, however, except the one to Ruth Schuyler. For the one to Randolph Schuyler was in Lowney's possession, and the one I had had from Vicky, and which was even then in my pocket, I had no intention of showing.

It was not necessary, however, for Fleming Stone said one was enough to gather all that he could learn from her chirography.

He studied it attentively, but only for a moment. Then he said, "A characteristic penmanship, but to me it only shows forcefulness, ingenuity and good nature. However, I'm not an expert, I only get a general impression, and the traits I've mentioned are undoubtedly to be found in the lady's nature. Are they not?" and he turned to me, as to one who knew.

"They are," I replied, "so far as I know Miss Van Allen. But my acquaintance with her is limited, and I can only agree superficially."

Stone eyed me closely, and I began to feel a little uncomfortable under his gaze. Clearly, I'd have to tell the truth, or incur his suspicion. Nor did I wish to prevaricate. I felt friendly toward poor little Vicky, and yet, I had no mind to run counter to the interest of Ruth Schuyler. The two sisters I didn't worry about, and indeed, they could look out for themselves. But Ruth Schuyler was in a position to demand justice, and if that justice accused Vicky Van, I must be honest and fair to both in my testimony.

Fleming Stone proceeded to question the women, more definitely and concisely now, and by virtue of his marvellous efficiency, he so shaped his inquiries, that he learned details with accuracy and rapidity.

It would never have occurred to me to ask the questions that he put, but as he went on, I saw their pertinence and value.

With Ruth's permission he called several of the servants and asked them a few things. Nothing of moment transpired, to my mind, but Stone was interested in a full account of where each servant was and what he was doing on the night of the murder. Each gave a straightforward and satisfactory account, and I realized that Stone was only getting a sense of the household atmosphere, and its relations to Mr. Schuyler himself.

Tibbetts, the middle-aged maid of Ruth Schuyler, told of the shock to her mistress when the news was brought.

"Mrs. Schuyler had retired," said Tibbetts, "at about ten o'clock, Mr. Schuyler was out, and was not expected home until late. I attended her, and after she was in bed, I went to bed myself."

"I'm told you do not live here," commented Stone, though in a disinterested way, and at the same time making notes of some other matters in his notebook.

"I have a room around on Third Avenue," replied Tibbetts. "I like a little home of my own, and when Mrs. Schuyler permits me, I go 'round there to sleep, and sometimes I go in the daylight hours. But on that night I happened to be staying here."

"Tibbetts is rather a privileged character," interposed Ruth. "She has been with me for many years, and as she likes a little place of her own, I adopted the plan of which she has told you."

"But that night you were here?" said Stone, to the maid.

"Yes, sir. I slept in Mrs. Schuyler's dressing room, as I always do when I'm here. Then when Jepson told me the—the awful news, I awoke Mrs. Schuyler and told her."

"Yes," said Stone. "I read all about that in the inquest report."

Chapter 14: Walls Have Tongues

"Now," said Fleming Stone, after he had learned all he desired from the Schuyler household, "now, if you please, I would like to go over the Van Allen house. You have the keys, Mr. Calhoun?"

"I have a latchkey to the street door." I replied, "the rooms are not locked."

I don't know why exactly, but I hated to have him go through Vicky Van's house. Of course, it must have been because she had begged me not to let Stone get into the case at all. But I hadn't been able to prevent that, the two Schuyler sisters being determined to have him. And I had no desire to impede justice or stand in the way of law and order, but, somehow or other, I felt the invasion of Vicky's home would bring about trouble for the girl, and my mind was filled with vague foreboding.

"We will go with you," announced Miss Rhoda. "I've wanted to see that house from the first. You'll go, Ruth?"

"Oh, no," and Ruth Schuyler shrank at the idea. "I've no wish to see the place where my husband was killed! How could you think of it? If I could do any good by going—"

"No, Mrs. Schuyler," said Fleming Stone, "you could do no good, and I quite understand why you would rather not go. The Misses Schuyler and Mr. Calhoun will accompany me, and we will start at once."

"Can't I go?" asked Winnie, who had come in recently, "I'm just crazy to see that house. You don't mind my going, do you, Ruth?"

"No, indeed, child. I'm perfectly willing."

Mr. Stone raised no objection, so Winnie went with us.

It was nearly five o'clock, full daylight, though the dusk was just beginning to fall. We went round to Vicky Van's and I opened the door for the party to enter.

The house had begun to show disuse. There was dust on the shining surfaces of the furniture and on the polished floors. The clocks had all stopped and the musty chill of a closed house was in the atmosphere.

"Ugh!" cried Winnie, "what a creepy feeling! And this house is too pretty to be so neglected! Why, it's a darling house. Look at that heavenly color scheme!"

Winnie had darted into the living-room, with its rose and gray appointments, and we all followed her.

"Don't touch anything, Miss Calhoun," cautioned Stone, and Win contented herself with gazing about, her hands clasped behind her.

The Schuyler sisters sniffed, and though they said little, they conveyed the idea that to their minds the bijou residence savored of reprehensible frivolity.

Fleming Stone lived up to his reputation as a detective, and scrutinized everything with quick, comprehensive glances. We went through the long living-room, and into the dining-room, whose pale green and silver again enchanted Winnie.

"The walls are exquisite," Stone agreed, looking closely at the panels of silk brocade, framed with a silver tracery.

"If walls have ears, they must burn at your praise," I said, in an effort to speak lightly, for Stone's face had an ominous look, as if he were learning grave truths.

"Walls not only have ears, they have tongues," he returned. "These walls have already told me much of Miss Van Allen's character."

"Oh, how?" cried Winnie, "do tell us how you deduce and all that!"

I looked hastily at Stone, thinking he might be annoyed by Winnie's volatile speech.

But he said kindly, "To the trained eye, Miss Calhoun, much is apparent that escapes the casual observer. But

you can understand that the taste displayed in the wall
decoration, shows a refined and cultured nature. A
woman of the adventuress type would prefer more garish
display. Of course, I am generalizing, but there is much to
bear me out. Then, I see, by certain tiny marks and
cracks, that these walls have lately been done over, and
that they were also redecorated another time not long
before. This proves that Miss Van Allen has money
enough to gratify her whims and she chooses to spend it
in satisfying her aesthetic preferences. Further, the walls
have been carefully cared for, showing an interested and
capable housekeeperly instinct and traits of extreme
orderliness and tidiness. Cleverness, even, for here, you
see, is a place, where a bit of the plaster has been defaced
by a knock or scratch, and it has been delicately painted
over with a little pale green paint which matches exactly.
It is not the work of a professional decorator, so reason
tells me that probably Miss Van Allen herself remedied
the defect."

"Good gracious!" exclaimed Winnie, "I can see all that
myself, now you tell me, but I never should have thought
of it! Tell me more."

"Then the pictures, which are so well chosen and
placed, that they seem part of the walls, are, as you
notice, all figure pieces. There are no landscapes. This, of
course, means that Miss Van Allen is not distinctly a
nature lover, but prefers humanity and society. This
argues for the joy of living and the appreciation of mental
pleasures and occupations. No devotee of nature would
have failed to have pictures of flowers or harmonizing
landscapes on these walls. So, you see, to be edified by
the tongues of walls, you must not only listen to them but
understand their language."

And then Stone began taking in the rest of the dining-
room's contents. The table, hastily cleared by the caterer's
men, was empty of the china and glass which they had
supplied, but still retained the candlesticks and epergnes

that were Vicky Van's own. These were of plated silver, not sterling, which fact Stone noted. The lace-trimmed linen, however, was of the finest and most elaborate sort. "An unholy waste of money!" declared Rhoda Schuyler, looking at the marvellous monogram of V. V. A. embroidered on the napkins.

But I gazed sadly at the table, only partially dismantled, which had been so gaily decked for Vicky's birthday supper.

Scanning the sideboard, Stone remarked the absence of the small carving knife. I told him I, too, had observed that, and that I had made search for it.

"Did you ask the caterer's people if they took it by mistake?" said the detective.

"No," I admitted, ashamed that I hadn't thought of it, and I promised to do so.

As Stone stood, silently contemplating the place where Randolph Schuyler had met his death, I stepped out into the hall. I had no conscious reason for doing so, but I did, and chancing to glance toward the stairs, I with difficulty repressed an exclamation.

For half-way up the staircase, I saw Vicky Van!

I was sure it was no hallucination, I positively saw her! She was leaning over the banister, listening to what Stone was saying. Suddenly, even as I looked, she ran upstairs and disappeared.

Was she safe? Could she escape? Perhaps by a back staircase, or could she manage to elude us and slip away somehow?

Then I was conscience-stricken. Was I conniving at the escape of a guilty person? Did I want to do this? I didn't know. Something told me I must tell Stone of her presence, and yet something else made it impossible for me to do so.

I turned back to the dining-room, and Miss Sarah was saying, "That's the spot, then, that's where Randolph was killed by that awful woman! Mr. Stone you must get her!

An eye for an eye—a life for a life! She must pay the penalty of her guilt!"

Winnie was listening, and tears stood in her eyes. Like Ruth Schuyler, from whom she doubtless took a cue, Win wasn't so ready to condemn Vicky Van unheard, as the two sisters were. She looked steadily at Fleming Stone, as if expecting him to produce Vicky then and there, and I quivered with the thought of what would happen if he knew that even at that moment Vicky was under the same roof with ourselves!

But Stone completed his survey of the dining-room, and as a matter of course, started next up the stairs. I pushed ahead a little, in my eagerness to precede him, but a vague desire to protect Vicky urged me on. I stood in the upper hall as the rest came up, and I imagined that Stone gave me a curious glance as he noted my evident embarrassment.

But Winnie dashed into the music room, and the Schuyler sisters quickly followed. Trust a woman to feel and show curiosity about her neighbor's home!

Again Stone examined the walls, but the immaculate white and gold sides of the music room said nothing intelligible to me, and if they spoke to him he did not divulge the message. The women exclaimed at the beautiful room, and, as Stone's examination here was short, we all filed back to Vicky's bedroom.

I heard no sound of her, and I breathed more freely, as we did not find her in bedroom or in the boudoir beyond. She had, then, succeeded in getting away, and trusted to me not to betray her presence there.

The boudoir or dressing-room, all pink satin and white enameled wicker called forth new exclamations from Winnie, and even Rhoda Schuyler expressed a grudging admiration.

"It is beautiful," she conceded. "I wish Ruth had come, after all. She loves this sort of furniture. Don't you remember, Sarah, she wanted Randolph to do up her dressing-room in wicker?"

"Yes, but he didn't like it, he said it was gim-crackery. And the Circassian walnut of Ruth's room is much handsomer."

"Of course it is. Ruth has a charming suite. Oh, do look at the dresses!"

Fleming Stone had flung open a wardrobe door, and the costumes disclosed, though not numerous, were of beautiful coloring and design. Winnie, unable to resist the temptation, fingered them lovingly, and called my attention to certain wonderful confections.

"What did she wear the night of the crime?" Stone asked, and I told him. Having Win for a sister, I am fairly good at describing women's clothes, and I drew a vivid word picture of Vicky's gold fringed gown.

"Heavenly!" exclaimed Winnie, although she had had me describe the gown to her on the average of twice a day for a week. "I wish I could see it! Some day, Chet, I'm going to have one like it."

"Fringe?" said Stone, curiously, "do women wear fringe nowadays?"

"Oh, yes," I responded. "But it was a long fringe of gilt beads that really formed an overdress to the tulle skirt. Stay, I've a piece of it," and I took out my pocketbook. "See, here it is. I found it caught in those gilded leaves at the lower corner of the mirror frame—that long dressing-mirror."

They all looked at the mirror, which hung flat against the wall; its foliated Florentine frame full of irregular protuberances.

"Of course," said Winnie, nodding her head, "I know just how she stood in front of it, whirling around to see her gown from all sides, like this." Win whirled herself around, before the glass, and succeeded in catching a bit of her own full skirt on the frame.

"You little goose!" I cried, as the fabric tore, "we don't need a demonstration at the expense of your frock!"

Fleming Stone was studying the strand of gold fringe. It was composed of tiny beads, of varying shapes, and had already begun to ravel into shreds.

"I'll keep this," he said, and willy-nilly, I lost my little souvenir of Vicky Van. But, of course, if he considered it evidence, I had to give it up, and the fact of doing so, partly salved my conscience of its guilty feeling at concealing the fact of Vicky's presence in her own house just then.

And, too, I said to myself, Mr. Stone is out to find her. Surely a detective of his calibre can accomplish that without help of an humble layman! So I kept my own counsel, and further search, of the next story, and later, of the basement rooms, gave no hint of Vicky's presence or departure.

Indeed, I began to wonder if I had really seen her. Could she have been so clearly in my mind, that I visualized her in a moment of clairvoyance? My reason rebelled at this, for I knew I saw her, as well as I knew I was alive. She had on the same little hat in which I had last seen her. She had on no cloak, and her tailor-made street dress was of a dark cloth. I couldn't be sure how she got away, for the basement door we found bolted on the inside, but she must have warily evaded and eluded us and slipped here and there as we pursued our course through the house, and then have gone out by the front door when we were, say, on the upper floors.

Returning to Vicky's boudoir, where her little writing-desk was, Fleming Stone began to run over the letters and papers therein.

It was locked, but he picked the flimsy fastening and calmly took up the task with his usual quick-moving, efficient manner.

I stayed with him, and the three women wandered back over the house again. He ran through letters with glancing quickness, flipped over sheafs of bills, and examined pens, ink and paper.

"There's so much that's characteristic about a desk," he said, as he observed the penwiper, stamps, pin-tray, and especially the pencils. "Indeed, I feel now that I know Miss Van Allen as well, if not better than you do yourself, Mr. Calhoun."

"In that case, then, you can't believe her guilty," I flashed back, for the very atmosphere of the dear little room made me more than ever Vicky's friend.

"But you see," and he spoke a bit sadly, "what I know of her is the real woman. I can't be deceived by her wiles and coquetries. I see only the actual traces of her actual self."

I knew what he meant, and there was some truth in it. For Vicky was a mystery, and I was not by any means sure, that she didn't hoodwink us when she chose to. Much as I liked and admired the girl, I was forced to believe she was not altogether disingenuous. And she was clever enough to hoodwink anybody. But if Stone's deductions were to be depended on, they were doubtless true evidence.

"Is she guilty?" I sighed.

"I can't say that, yet, but I've found nothing that absolutely precludes her guilt. On the contrary, I've found things, which if she is guilty, will go far toward proving it."

This sounded a bit enigmatical, but Stone was so serious, that I grasped his general meaning and let it go at that.

"I mean," he said, divining my thoughts, "that things may or may not be evidence according to the guilt or innocence of the suspect. If you find a little boy in the pantry beside an empty jampot, you suspect him of stealing jam. Now, if lots of other circumstances prove that child did take the jam, the empty pot is evidence. But, if circumstances develop that convince you the child did not have any jam whatever, that day, then the jampot is no evidence at all."

"And you have found empty jampots?" I asked.

"I have. But, so far, I'm not sure that they are condemnatory evidence. Though, in justice to my own work, I must add, that they have every appearance of being so."

"You already like Vicky Van, then," I said, quickly, moved to do so, by a certain note of regret in his voice.

"No man could help liking a woman who possesses her traits. She has delightful taste and tastes. She is most charitable, her accounts show sums wisely expended on worthy charities. And letters from friends prove her a truly loyal and lovable character."

"Such a girl couldn't kill a man!" I broke out.

"Don't say that. There is no one incapable of crime. But such a nature would require very strong provocation and desperate conditions. These granted, it is by no means impossible. Now, I am through for to-day, but, if you please I will keep the key of the house. As the case is now in my hands, you will not object?"

"No," I said, a little reluctantly. For suppose Vicky should give me another commission or ask me to perform another errand in the house.

"You have a transparent face, Mr. Calhoun," and Fleming Stone smiled quizzically. "Why do you want to keep the key?"

"My aunt is most desirous of seeing this house," I deliberately prevaricated, "and I thought—"

But I didn't deceive the astute detective. "No, that isn't it," he said, quietly. "I'm not sure, but I think you are in touch with Miss Van Allen."

"And if I am?" I flared up.

"Very well," he returned, "it is, as you imply, none of my business. But I want to know your attitude, and if it is antagonistic to my work, I am sorry, but I will conduct my course accordingly."

"Mr. Stone," I confessed, "I am not antagonistic, but I do know a little about Miss Van Allen's movements that I haven't told. I cannot see that it would assist you in any way to know it—"

"That's enough," and Fleming Stone spoke heartily. "Your assurance of that is sufficient. Now, are we working together?"

I hesitated. Then I suddenly thought of Ruth Schuyler. I owed her a business fealty, and somehow I liked to feel that I also owed her a personal allegiance, and both these demanded my efforts to avenge the death of her husband, irrespective of where the blow might fall.

So I said, honestly, "We are, Mr. Stone. I will help you, if I can, and if at any time I think my withheld information will help you, I will make it known. Is that satisfactory?"

"Entirely so," and the handshake that Stone gave me was like a signed and sealed bond, to which I tacitly but none the less truthfully subscribed.

CHAPTER 15: FIBSY

Next morning as I started for my office, I found myself combating a strong impulse to call in at Ruth Schuyler's. I had no errand there, and I knew that if she required my services she would summon me. It was no longer incumbent on me to try to unravel the murder mystery. Fleming Stone had that matter in charge, and his master-mind needed no assistance from me.

And yet, I wanted to stop at the Fifth Avenue house, if only for a moment, to reassure myself of Ruth's well-being. Though above me in social rank, the little widow seemed to me a lonely and pathetic woman, and I knew she had begun to depend on me for advice and sympathy. Of course, she could turn to Fleming Stone, but, in a way, he was adviser of the Schuyler sisters, and I knew Ruth hesitated to intrude on his time.

I was still uncertain whether to call or not, and as I walked along the few feet between my own house and the Avenue, I crossed the street as I reached Vicky Van's house, and naturally looked at it as I passed.

And after I had passed the flight of brownstone steps, and was going along by the iron fence, I turned to look at the area door. This was my performance every morning, and always without thought of seeing anything of importance.

But this time the area door stood half-way open, and looking out was a boy, a red-headed chap, with a freckled face and bright, wise eyes.

I turned quickly and went in at the area gate.

"Who are you?" I demanded, "and what are you doing here?"

"I'm Fibsy," he said, as if that settled it.

"Fibsy who?" I asked, but I dropped my indignant tone, for the lad seemed to be composedly sure of his rights there.

"Aw, jest Fibsy. That's me name, because, if you want to know, because I'm a natural born liar and I fib for a living."

He was impudent without being offensive; his wide smile was good-natured and the twinkle in his eye a friendly one.

"I got yer number," he said, after a comprehensive survey of my person, "you're C. Calhoun. Ain't you?"

"I sure am," I agreed, meeting his taste for the vernacular, "and now for your real name."

"Terence McGuire," he smiled, and with a quick gesture he snatched off his cap. "C'mon in, if you like. I'm F. Stone's right-hand man."

"What!" I cried, in amazement.

"Yep, that's what. I'm—well, I like to call myself his caddy. I follow him round, and hold his clues for him, till he wants one, then I hand it out. See?"

"Not entirely. But I gather you're in Mr. Stone's employ."

"You bet I am! And I'm on me job twenty-four hours a day."

"And what is your job just now?"

"Well, since eight A.M. I've been holdin' up this door, waitin' for yer honor to pass by. An' I got you, didn't I?"

"Yes, I'm here." I stepped inside and the boy closed the door. We went into the front basement room, where there was a lighted gas stove.

"I camp here, 'count o' the heats. There's no use gettin' up the steam fer the few casual callers that drops in at present. Now, Mr. Calhoun, I don't want to be stuffy nor nuthin', but Mr. Stone said I might ask you some few things, if I liked an' you can answer or not, as you like. This ain't no orficial investigation, but I s'pose you're as intrusted as anybody in findin' this here Victoria Van Allen?"

"I'm interested in finding the murderer of Mr. Schuyler," I replied.

"An' maybe they ain't one an' the same. That's so." He spoke thoughtfully and scanned my face with a quizzical glance. "But, of course, Mr. Stone'll find out. Now, Mr. Calhoun, if you don't mind, will you give me a line on that maid person, that Julia?"

"Julie, she is called."

"All right, Julie goes. Is she a young thing?"

"No; just this side of middle-aged. Probably thirty-five or so."

"Good looker?"

"Why, about average. Brown hair, brownish eyes—really, I never noticed her closely enough to think about her appearance. She is, I'm sure, a good servant and devoted to Miss Van Allen."

"But don't you know anything special? Anything that would pick her out from a lot of other good servants?"

"In appearance, you mean?"

"Yes."

"I can't think of anything. Let me see. She wears glasses—"

"What sort?"

"I don't know. Just ordinary glasses, I guess."

"Spectacles or nose-riders?"

"I'm not sure. Spectacles, I think. And she has a great many gold-filled teeth."

"Front ones?"

"Yes, that is, they're very noticeable when she speaks to you."

"Well, that's sumpum. Is she quick and spry-like, or poky?"

I smiled at the boy's eagerness. "She's rather alert," I said, "but, of course, quiet and respectful. I never looked at her with any personal interest, so I can only give you my general impressions."

"You see, it's this way," and the boy looked very serious, "wherever Miss Van Allen is, that Julie's there, too. And when Miss Van Allen wants errands done, of course, she sends Julie. And, of course, said Julie is disguised. I dope out all this has to be so. For Miss Van Allen has mailed letters and—oh, well, of course she could mail letters in lots of ways, but sumpum tells me, that she depends on Miss Julie as an errand girl. So, I want to find out the look of the Julie person, and see if I can't track her down, and so get at Miss Van Allen. Vicky Van, I believe her friends call her."

"They do," said I, looking sternly at the boy, "and I'll say right here, that I'm one of her friends, and I won't stand for any impertinence or any remarks of any sort about that lady. If she is suspected of this crime, let the law take its course, but until there is some direct evidence, don't you dare to connect her name with it."

"I'm only obeying Mr. Stone's orders. And, take it from me, Mr. Calhoun, I ain't so fresh as to make remarks about a lady. I'm a prevaricator of the truth, but only when it's abserlutely necessary. And on the other hand, I'm a born protector of women. Why, I'd be only too tickled to find a gentleman suspect. Or, at least, to clear Miss Van Allen from all s'picion."

"Why do you feel such a kindly interest in the lady?"

"This house, for one reason. You see, I've been all over it, at Mr. Stone's orders, and I ree'lize what a nice lady she is. I don't have to see her, to understand her tastes and her 'complishments. Why, jest the books on her centre tables and the records for her phonograph spell her out for me, in words of one syllable. And, though I'm hunting for her, it isn't with a solid hunch that's she's the knife-sticker. Not by no means. But find her I've gotto! Because F. Stone says for me to."

I looked at the boy more curiously. He was a strange admixture of street boy and sleuth. His quick, darting eyes were never still, but warily alert to catch the meaning of any sound or motion on my part. I felt as if he read me through, and would not have been surprised to have him tell me he knew of my recent communications with Vicky. But I only said, "You are, then, Mr. Stone's right-hand man?"

"I put it that way, yes. But really, I'm his apprentice, and I'm learning his trade. I study his methods, and I add some gumption of my own, and if I can help him, I'm glad and happy. And anyway, I'm learning."

"And this talk about your lying? Is that straight goods?"

"If it is, how can you believe what I tell you?" he asked, whimsically. "But, I used to be a fierce liar. Then, gettin' in with F. Stone, made me see it's wrong to lie— usuerly, that is. So I don't, now—leastways, not much. Only when it's jest the only thing to do to save game."

"How does Mr. Stone know when you're telling the truth, then?"

"Good land, I don't lie to him! I wouldn't, and if I did, it wouldn't be any use. He'd see through me, quicker'n scat! But, honest, I wouldn't. You see, he's my idol, yes sir, my idol, that's what that man is! Well, Mr. Calhoun, as you've told me all you can pry loose from your stock of infermation, you an' me may as well make our adooses."

"How do you know I haven't revealed all I know of the case?"

"Oh, I read from your mobile counternance that you're keepin' sumpum back, but it don't matter. F. Stone'll nail it, when he gets good an' ready. What I wanted from you was mostly the speakin' likeness of the Julie dame. An' I guess I got it. Oh, say, one other thing. Who among Miss Van Allen's friends is an artist?"

"Miss Gale is one. Miss Ariadne Gale."

"Thank you, sir. And will you gimme her address?"

I did so, and then I went away, thinking Fleming Stone a queer sort of detective to have for assistant such an illiterate, uncultured boy as Fibsy. The name was enough to condemn him! But as I thought the little chap over, I realized that his talk had been clear-headed and to the point, besides showing sagacity and perspicacity.

It was growing late, but after this interview I felt I must see Ruth for a few minutes, so called at the Schuyler house.

She greeted me cordially and seemed glad to see me. Winnie was still acting as secretary for her, but the rush of notes of condolence was over, and as Ruth was not, of course, giving or accepting social invitations, there was not so much work for Win as at first. But the two had become fast friends, and Winnie told me how they sat together chatting often for pleasant half hours at a time.

I told Ruth about the strange boy at Vicky Van's house.

"Yes," she said, "I've heard about him. Mr. Stone picked him up somewhere and he uses him as a sort of outside scout. He has all confidence in him, though I believe the little chap rejoices in the name of Fibber."

"Fibsy," I corrected. "He is certainly a bright youth. And he plans to hunt down Miss Van Allen by means of her maid, Julie."

"Are they together?"

"We only suppose so. It seems probable, that Miss Van Allen would want the help, if not the protection of her servant. Julie is a most capable woman, and devoted to her mistress."

"I've heard so. I have a kind, thoughtful woman, too, and I should miss her terribly were I without her."

"Oh, but your Tibbetts is a servant, and nothing more. This Julie was a real friend to Miss Van Allen, and looked after her in every way. Housekeeper, maid, nurse, and general bodyguard."

"Yes, Miss Van Allen must have needed such a person, since, as I am told, she lived alone. My sisters-in-law are quite in love with the Van Allen house. Both they and Winnie have been singing its praises this morning. It seems your Vicky Van is a lady of most refined tastes."

"She certainly is. I can't help thinking if you and she had known each other, in favorable circumstances, you would have been friends."

"It may be. I have never felt sure that she is the guilty one, but I have changed my mind about not wanting her to be found. I do want that she should be. Mr. Schuyler's sisters have shown me that to hesitate at or neglect any means of hunting her out would be wrong. And so, I am glad we have Mr. Stone and I hope he will succeed in his search."

"What changed your mind, especially?"

"I realized that it would be disloyalty to my husband's memory to let his possible slayer go free. The girl must be found, and then if she can be freed of suspicion, very well, but the case must be investigated fully."

"I dare say you are right. Mr. Schuyler was a man of importance and influence, and aside from that, every deed of blood calls for revenge. I honor you for deciding as you have."

"It is justice that moves me, more than my personal inclination," Ruth went on. "I will not deny, Mr. Calhoun, that in some ways, my husband's death has freed me from certain restrictions that hampered and galled me. I shouldn't mention this to you, but I know the sisters have told you that I have, in many ways, gone counter to Mr. Schuyler's wishes, since I have been my own mistress. It is true. He and I disagreed greatly on matters of the household and matters of my personal comfort and convenience. Now that I can do so, I am arranging my life differently. It is natural that I should do this, but the Schuyler ladies think that I have begun indecently soon. I say this, not by way of apology, but because I want you to understand."

Ruth looked very sweet and wistful, as she seemed to make a bid for my sympathy. I was impressed anew by the soft pallor of her face and the sweet purity of her gray eyes. I contrasted her with Vicky Van. One, the embodiment of life and gayety, the other a gentle, dovelike personality, which, however, hinted sometimes at hidden fires. I believed that Ruth Schuyler had been so repressed, so dominated by her brute of a husband, that her nature had never expanded to its own possibilities.

And, like a blinding flash of lightning, the knowledge came to me that I loved her! It was no uncertain conviction. The fact sprang full-armed, to my brain, and my heart swelled with the bliss of it.

I scarcely dared look at her. I couldn't tell her—yet. I had no reason to think she cared for me, other than as the merest acquaintance, yet, then and there, I vowed to myself that she should care.

I thought of Vicky Van—poor little Vicky. She had interested me—did interest me, but in only a friendly way. Indeed, my interest in her was prompted by sympathy for her luckless position and the trust she had reposed in me, I would hold her trust sacred. I would never play false to Vicky Van. But henceforth and forever my heart and soul belonged to my liege lady, my angel-faced Ruth.

"What is the matter, Mr. Calhoun?" I heard her saying, and I looked up to see her smiling almost gayly at me. "Your thoughts seem to be a thousand miles away!"

"Oh, not so far as that," I protested. Somehow, I felt buoyantly happy. I had no wish to tell her of my love, at present I was quite content to worship her in secret, and I exulted in a sort of clairvoyant knowledge that I should yet win her. I smiled into her dear eyes, as I continued: "They were really round the corner in Vicky Van's house."

To my delight she pouted a little. "Let's talk of something else," she said. "I've no doubt Miss Van Allen is charming, and her home a perfect gem, but I own up I'm not anxious to discuss her all the time and with every one."

"You shall be exempt from it with me," I promised. "Henceforth her name is taboo between us, and you shall choose our subjects yourself."

"Then let's talk about me. Now, you know, Mr. Calhoun, I never see Mr. Bradbury, so you must be my legal adviser in all my quandaries. First, and this is a serious matter, I don't want to continue to live with the Schuyler ladies. We are diametrically opposed on all matters of opinion, and disagree on many matters of fact." Ruth smiled, and I marveled afresh at the way her face lighted up when she indulged in that little smile of hers. "Nor," she went on, "do they want to live with me. So, it ought to be an easy matter to please us all. As to the house and furnishings, they are all mine, but if the sisters prefer to live here, and let me go elsewhere, I am willing to give them the house and its contents."

"I know you don't care for this type of residence," I said, "indeed, Miss Schuyler said yesterday, as we looked over Vicky Van's house, that it was just the sort of thing you liked."

"Oh, I can't think I would like her house! I supposed it was a plain little affair. Harmonious and pretty, Winnie says, but she didn't give me the impression it was elaborate."

"No, it isn't. And it wouldn't be as grand as your home ought to be. But mention of the girl is not allowed, I believe—"

She smiled again, and resumed: "Well, I want you to sound the Schuyler sisters, and find out their wishes. When I speak to them, they only say for me to wait until after the mystery is solved and all this horrid publicity and notoriety at an end. But I want to go away from them now. I want Mr. Stone to do his work, and I hope he will find that girl and all that, but I can't stand it to live in this atmosphere of detectives and reporters and policemen any longer than I must. Would it do for me to go to some quiet hotel for a while? I could take Tibbetts, and just be quietly by myself, while the Schuylers continue to live in this house."

I thought it over. I understood perfectly how she hated to be questioned continually as to her life with her late husband, for I was beginning to realize that that life had been a continuous tragedy. Nothing much definite, but many sidelights and stray hints had shown me how he had treated her, and how patiently she had borne it. And, now he was gone, and I, for one, didn't blame her that she wanted to get away from the scenes of her slavery to him. For it had been that. He had enforced his ideas and opinions upon her, until she had been allowed to do nothing and to have nothing as she wished.

And now, she desired only peace and quietness somewhere, anywhere, away from the two who represented Randolph Schuyler's tyranny and carping criticism without his right to obtrude them on her.

"I will speak to them," I said, "and I'm sure we can arrange some mode of life for you which will give you rest and freedom of judgment."

"Oh, if you only can!" she murmured, as she held out a friendly hand.

CHAPTER 16: A FUTILE CHASE

It was Sunday afternoon, and we were in conclave in the Schuyler library. Fleming Stone was summing up his results of the past few days and, though it was evident he had done all that mortal man could do, yet he had no hint or clue as to where Vicky Van might be.

And, he held, that nothing else was of consequence compared to this knowledge. She must be found, and whether that could be done quickly, by search or by chance, or whether it would take a long time of waiting, he could not say. He felt sure, that she must disclose herself, sooner or later, but if not, and if their search continued unavailing, then he held out no hope for success.

"It's a unique case," he said, "in my experience. All depends on finding that woman. If she is innocent, herself, she knows who did it. And, if she is the guilty one, she is clever enough to remain hidden. It may be she is miles away, out of the country, perhaps. She has had ample time to make arrangements to go abroad, or to any distant place. Her guilt seems to me probable, because she has literally abandoned her house and her belongings. An innocent woman would scarcely leave all those modern and valuable furnishings unless for some very strong reason. But as to finding her—a needle in a haystack presents an easy problem by contrast!"

"Doubtless she is hiding in the house of some friend," suggested Ruth, thoughtfully. "It seems to me she must have been taken in and cared for by some one who loved her, that night she disappeared."

"I think so, too," agreed Stone. "But I've been to see all her friends that I can find out about. I've called on a score of them, finding their addresses in her address book that

Mr. Lowney gave me. Of course, they may have been deceiving me, but I feel safe in asserting that she is not under the protection of any one I interviewed. She returned to her house last Monday night, the police believe, for the purpose of getting her mail. This shows a daring almost unbelievable! That mail must have been of desperate importance to her. She has not been to the house since, they feel sure, and since I have been on the case she could not have entered, for I have kept it under strict surveillance. I think she will never return to it. Presumably she got the letters she was so anxious for. Her mail, that has arrived the last few days, I have not opened, but the envelopes show mostly tradesmen's cards, or are indubitably social correspondence. There seem to be no letters from lawyers or financial firms. However, if nothing develops, I shall open the letters. This case, being unprecedented, necessitates unusual proceedings."

"I'm disappointed in you, Mr. Stone," said Rhoda Schuyler, testily; "I didn't suppose you were superhuman, but I did think, with your reputation and all, you would be able to find that woman. I've heard say that nobody could absolutely vanish in New York City, and not be traced."

"You don't regret my so-far failure a bit more than I do, Miss Schuyler, but I feel no shame or embarrassment over it. Nor am I ready to admit myself beaten. I have a theory, or, rather a conviction that there is one and only one explanation of this strange affair. I am not quite ready to expound this, but in a day or two I shall find if it is the true solution, and if so I shall soon find Miss Van Allen."

"I knew you would," and Sarah Schuyler nodded her head, in satisfaction. "I told Rhoda to give you more time and you would not disappoint us. All right, Mr. Stone, use all the time you need. But no Schuyler must remain unavenged. I want to see that woman killed—yes, killed, for her murder of my brother."

Sarah Schuyler looked like a figure of Justice herself, as, with flashing eyes she declared her wrath. And it was her right. Her brother's blood called out for vengeance. But the more gentle-souled Ruth shuddered and shrank from this stern arraignment.

"Oh, Sarah," she murmured, "not killed! Don't condemn a woman to that!"

"Why not, Ruth? If a woman can kill, a woman should be killed. But she won't be," she added, bitterly. "No jury ever convicts a woman, no matter how clearly her guilt is proven."

Just then Fibsy appeared. He was a strange little figure, and showed a shy awkwardness at the grandeur of his surroundings. He bobbed a funny little curtsy to Ruth, whom he already adored, and with an embarrassed nod, included the rest of us in a general greeting.

Then to Fleming Stone he said, in an eager, triumphant tone, "I got 'em!"

"Got what?" asked Ruth, smiling at him.

"Got pictures of Miss Van Allen, and Julie, too."

"What!" cried Ruth, interested at once; "let me see them."

Fibsy glanced at her and then at Stone, and handed a parcel to the latter.

"He's my boss," the boy said, as if by way of apology for slighting her request.

Fleming Stone opened the parcel and showed two sketches.

"Miss Gale made them," he explained. "I sent Fibsy over there to induce her to give us at least a hint of Miss Van Allen's personal appearance. The boy could wheedle it from her, when I couldn't. See?"

He handed the pictures to Miss Rhoda, for he, too, respected authority, but we all gathered round to look.

They were the merest sketches. A wash of water-color, but they showed merit. As the only one present who knew Vicky Van, I was asked of the truth of their portraiture.

"Fairly good," I said, "yes, more than that. This of Vicky shows the coloring of her face and hair and the general effect of her costume, more than her actual physiognomy. But it is certainly a close enough likeness to make her recognizable if you find her."

And this was true. Ariadne had caught the sidelong glance of Vicky Van's dark-lashed eyes, and the curve of her scarlet lips. The coloring was perfect, just Vicky's vivid tints, and the dark hair, looped over her ears, was as she always wore it. Ariadne had drawn her in the gown she had worn that fatal evening, and the women eagerly scrutinized the gorgeous costume.

"No wonder those long strands of fringe caught in that scraggly mirror frame!" exclaimed Winnie, who never missed a point.

"Right," said Stone. "If she whirled around as you did, Miss Calhoun, it's a wonder she didn't spoil her whole gown."

The pose and the figure were not exactly Vicky's. Ariadne wasn't much on catching a likeness or a physical effect. But the color and atmosphere were fine, and I told this to Stone, who agreed that it was a decided help in the search.

Julie's portrait was the same. Not a real likeness of the woman, but an impressionist transcript of her salient points. The gray gown and white apron, the thick-rimmed glasses, the parted lips, showing slightly protruding teeth, the plainly parted brown hair, all were the real Julie; and yet, except for these accessories I'm not sure I could have recognized the subject of the sketch. However, as I told Stone, it certainly was a helpful indication of the sort of woman he was to look for, and even in disguise, the physical characteristics must show.

The detective was positive that wherever Vicky Van and Julie were, or whatever they were doing, they were in all probability disguised, and thoroughly so, or they must have been discovered ere this.

To my amusement, Fibsy and Ruth were holding a tete-a-tete conversation. The kind-hearted woman had, doubtless, felt sorry for the boy's shyness, and had drawn him into chat to put him at his ease.

She had succeeded, too, for he was animated, and had lost his self-consciousness under the charm of her smile.

"And I'll bet your birthday comes in the spring," he was saying, as I caught the tenor of their talk.

"It does," said Ruth, looking surprised. "How did you guess?"

"'Cause you're just like a little spring flower—a white crocus or a bit of arbutus."

And then, noting my attention, the boy was covered with confusion and blushed to the tips of his ears. He rose from where he sat, and shuffled awkwardly around the great room, devoting exaggerated attention to some books in the glassed cases, and twirling his fingers in acute embarrassment.

"You scared him away," chided Ruth, under her breath, as our glances met. "He and I were getting positively chummy."

"Why was he talking of your birthday? I asked.

"I don't know, I'm sure. He said I was born in the spring, because I'm like a flower! Really, that child will grow up a poet, if he doesn't look out!"

"You are like a flower," I murmured back. "And I'm glad your birthday is in spring. I mean to celebrate it!"

And then I thought of poor Vicky Van's birthday, so tragically ended, and I quickly changed the subject.

Armed with the pictures, Fleming Stone and his young assistant spent the next day on a still hunt.

And in the evening Stone came over to see me.

"A little quiet confab," he said, as we secluded ourselves in my sitting-room and closed the door, "I've been to a score of places, and invariably they recognize Miss Van Allen and her maid, but all say they've not seen her since the tragedy. I went to shops, offices, the bank and places where she would be likely to need to go. Also, her friends' houses. But nothing doing. The shops have heard from her, in the way of paid bills, checks and such matters, but I learned absolutely nothing that throws any light on her whereabouts. Now, Mr. Calhoun, the very thoroughness of her disappearance, the very inviolable secrecy of her hiding-place proves to me that she isn't hiding."

"Now, Mr. Stone," I said, smiling, "you talk like a real story-book detective. Cryptic utterances of that sort are impressive to the layman, you know."

"Pshaw!" and he looked annoyed, "if you knew anything about detective work, you'd know that the most seemingly impossible conditions are often the easiest to explain."

"Well, then, explain. I'll be glad to hear."

"I will. And, in return, Mr. Calhoun, I'm going to ask you if you don't think, that all things considered, you ought to tell me what you are keeping back? You won't mind, will you, if I say that I have deduced, from evidence," he smiled, "that your interests are largely coincident with those of Mrs. Schuyler?"

"You're on," I said, shortly, but not annoyed at his perspicacity.

"Well, then, I assure you that Mrs. Schuyler is most desirous of locating Miss Van Allen. She is not so revengeful or vituperative as the sisters of her husband, but she feels it is due to her husband's memory to find his slayer, if possible. Now suppose you tell me what you know, and I promise to keep it an inviolate confidence except so far as it actually helps the progress of the wheels of justice."

"I do want to do what is best for Mrs. Schuyler's interests," I said, after I had thought a moment. "But, I must confess, I have a certain sympathy and pity for Victoria Van Allen. I cannot believe her guilty—"

"Then tell me frankly the truth. If you are right, and she is not the murderer, the truth can't harm her. And if she is the guilty person, you are compounding a felony, in the eyes of the law, to withhold your information."

Stone spoke a little sternly, and I realized he was right. If Vicky were untraceably hidden, all I could tell wouldn't hurt her. And, too, I couldn't see that it would, anyway. Moreover, as Stone said, I was making myself amenable to the law, by a refusal to tell all I knew, and since I was so aware of my own devotion to Ruth Schuyler, I felt I had no right to do anything that she would disapprove. And, I knew that a touch of feminine pique in her disposition would resent any consideration of Vicky over her own claims!

Therefore, I told Fleming Stone all I knew of Victoria Van Allen, both before, during and after the occasion of her birthday party.

He listened, with his deep eyes fixed on my face.

"Most extraordinary!" he said, at last, after I had finished. "I never heard of such daring! To enter her own house when it was watched by the police—"

"Only the post patrol, then," I reminded him. "She could easily manage between his rounds."

"Yes, yes, I know. But you've put the whole thing in different focus. Tell me more."

There was no more to tell, but I went over my story again, amplifying and remembering further details, until we had spent the whole evening. He egged me on by questions and his burning, eager eyes seemed to drink in my words as if they were so much priceless wisdom.

And I told him, too, that I had promised to put Vicky's address book in the Chinese jar for her that very evening.

"We'll do it!" he exclaimed, promptly. "She meant to meet you there, I'm sure, but I'm also sure she changed her mind about that, when she learned of my advent. However, we'll keep your promise."

Acting at his instructions, I went with him over to Vicky Van's. It was about midnight, and as he had the address book with him, he kept possession of it.

We went in the house, and in the dark, felt our way up to the music room. Stone put the book in the jar, and motioned for me to hide behind a sofa. He himself took up his vigil behind a window-curtain, of heavy brocade.

He had planned all this, before we left my house, and no word was spoken as we took our places. His hope was that Vicky would come into the house late and go straight for her book and quickly out again. He had directed me to wait until she had really abstracted the book from the jar and then, as she was leaving the room, spring after her and stop her.

I obeyed orders implicitly, and, as Stone had warned me, we had a bit of a wait. I grew cramped and tired, and at last I gave up all hope of Vicky's appearance.

And then, she came!

Silently, absolutely without sound, she glided in from the hall. My eyes, now accustomed to the semi-gloom of the room, could discern her figure as it approached the great vase. Softly, she raised the cover, she abstracted the book, and with noiseless touch was replacing the cover, when she threw back her head, as if she sensed our presence. I had made no move, nor had I heard a breath of sound from Stone, but Vicky knew some one was present. I knew that by her startled movement. She gave a stifled scream, and pushing the great jar off on the floor, where it crashed to pieces, she rushed out of the room and down stairs.

"After her, Calhoun! Fly!" shouted Stone, and as he flung back the heavy curtains the street lights illuminated the scene. But as we avoided the broken fragments we bumped together and lost a few seconds in our recovery from the impact.

This gave Vicky a start, and we heard the street door slam as we raced down the stairs. Here, too, we lost a second or two, for I stepped back to give Stone space just as he did the same for me, and when we had reached the foot of the stairs, leaped through the hall, wrenched open the door and dashed down the steps to the pavement, we saw the flying figure of Vicky Van round the Fifth Avenue corner, and turn South.

After her we ran, as fast as mortal man can run, I verily believe, and when we reached the Avenue there was no one in sight!

Stone stood stock-still, looking down the street.

The Avenue was lighted, as usual, and we could see a block and more in both directions, but no sign of Vicky. Nor was there a pedestrian abroad, or a motor. The Avenue was absolutely uninhabited, as far as our eyes could reach.

"Where'd she go?" I panted.

"Into some house, or, maybe, hiding in an area. We must search them all, but very warily. She's a witch, a wonder-woman, but all the same, the earth didn't open and swallow her!"

We searched every area way on the block. One of us would go in and explore while the other stood guard. The third house was the Schuyler residence, but Stone also searched thoroughly in its basement entrance.

"All dark and locked up," he reported, as he came out from there. "And, of course, she wouldn't seek sanctuary there! But I've wondered if she isn't concealed in one of these nearby houses, as she has such ready access to her own home."

But it was impossible. Every basement entrance was locked and bolted for the night and all the windows were dark.

"She's given us the slip," said Stone, in deep chagrin. "But perhaps she crossed the street. Maybe she didn't run down this side very far. Let's go over."

We crossed and looked over the stone wall of the park. Surely Vicky Van had not had time to scramble over that wall before we reached the corner. It had been not more than a few seconds after we saw her flying form turn down the Avenue, and she couldn't have crossed the street and scaled the wall in that time!

Where was she? What had become of her?

"Ring up the houses and inquire," I suggested. "You're justified in doing that."

"No use," he responded. "If she was expected they won't give her away, and if she isn't there, they'd be pretty angry at our intrusion. I'll admit, Calhoun, I've never been so mystified in my life!"

"Nor I!" I emphatically agreed.

Chapter 17: The Gold-Fringed Gown

After that night Fleming Stone became more desperately in earnest in his search for Vicky. It seemed as if the sight of her, the realization that she was a real woman and not a myth, had whetted his eagerness to discover her hiding place and bring her to book.

He established himself in her house, and both he and Fibsy practically lived there, going out for their meals or picnicking in the basement room. This room became his headquarters, and a plain clothes man was on duty whenever Stone and Fibsy were both absent.

"Though I don't think she'll ever come back again," Stone declared, gloomily. "She was desperately anxious for that address book, and so she got it, through my stupidity. I might have known she'd make a dash for the street door. I should have had that exit guarded. But I've seen her, and I'll get her yet! At any rate she hasn't left the country, or hadn't last night, whatever she may do to-day."

It was the day after Vicky had given us the slip. It was midafternoon, and I had gone to see Stone, on my return from my office. I was sadly neglecting my own business nowadays, but Mr. Bradbury looked after it, and he sanctioned my devotion to the Schuyler cause.

"Randolph Schuyler was an important citizen," he said, "and his murderer must be apprehended if possible. Do all you can, Calhoun, for humanity's sake and the law's. Take all the time you want to, I'll see to your important business."

So, though I went downtown every morning, I came back at noon or soon after and plunged afresh into the work of finding Vicky Van.

There was little I could do, but Stone consulted and questioned me continually as to Vicky's habits or pursuits, and I told him frankly all I knew.

Also I managed to make business matters loom up so importantly as to necessitate frequent calls on Ruth Schuyler, and I spent most of my afternoon hours in the Fifth Avenue house.

And Ruth was most kind to me. I couldn't say she showed affection or even especial interest, but she turned to me as a confidant and we had many long, pleasant conversations when the subject of the mystery was not touched upon.

Though she never said a word against Randolph Schuyler, I couldn't help learning that, aside from the horror of it, his death was to her a blessed relief. He had not been a good man, nor had he been a good husband. On the contrary, he had blighted Ruth's whole life by thwarting her every innocent desire for gayety or pleasure.

For instance, she spoke of her great enjoyment of light opera or farce comedy, but as Mr. Schuyler didn't care for such entertainment he had never allowed her to go. He had a box at the Grand Opera, and Ruth loved to go, but she liked lighter music also.

This was not told complainingly, but transpired in the course of a conversation at which Fibsy chanced to be present.

"Gee!" he said, looking at Ruth commiseratingly, "ain't you never heard 'The Jitney Girl' or 'The Prince of Peoria'?"

Ruth shook her head, smiling at the boy's amazement. There was a subtle sympathy between these two that surprised me, for Ruth Schuyler was fastidious in her choice of friends. But he amused her, and he was never really impertinent—merely naive and unconventional.

Well, on the day I speak of, Stone and I sat in the basement room awaiting Fibsy's return. He was out after certain information and we hoped much from it.

"I gotta bunch o' dope," he announced, as he suddenly appeared before us. "Dunno 's it'll pan out much, but listen 'n' I'll spill a earful."

I had learned that Fibsy, or Terence, as we ought to call him, was trying to discard his street slang, and was succeeding fairly well, save in moments of great excitement or importance. And so, I hoped from his slangy beginning, that he had found some fresh data.

"I chased up that chore boy first," he related, "an' he didn't know anything at all. Said Miss Van Allen's a lovely lady, but he 'most never saw her, the Julie dame did all the orderin' an' payin' s'far's he was concerned. Good pay, but irregular work. She'd be here a day or two, an' then like's not go 'way for a week. Well, we knew that before. Then, next, I tracked to his lair the furnace man. Same story. Here to-day an' gone to-morrer, as the song says. 'Course, he ain't only a stoker, he's really an odd job man—ashes, sidewalks, an' such. Well, he didn't help none—any, I mean. But," and the shock of red hair seemed to bristle with triumph, "I loined one thing! That Julie has been to the sewing woman and the laundress lady and shut 'em up! Yes, sir! that's what she's done!"

"Tell it all," said Stone, briefly.

"Well, I struck the seamstress first. She wouldn't tell a thing, and I said, calmly, 'I know Julie paid you to keep your mouth shut, but if you don't tell, the law'll make you!' That scared her. and she owned up that Julie was to see her 'bout a week ago and give her fifty dollars not to tell anything at all whatsomever about Miss Van Allen! Some girl, that Vicky Van!"

"Julie went there herself!" I cried.

"Yep. The real Julie, gold teeth and all. But I quizzed the needle pusher good and plenty, and she don't know much of evidential value."

It was always funny when Fibsy interlarded his talk with legal phrases, but he was unconscious of any incongruity and went on:

"You see, as I dope it out, she's accustomed to sit in Miss Van Allen's boodore a-sewin' an' might have overheard some gossip or sumpum like that, an' Miss Van Allen was afraid she'd scatter it, an' so she sent Julie to shut her up. I don't believe the woman knows where Miss Van is now."

"I must see her," said Stone.

"Yes, sir. She won't get away. She's a regular citizen, an' respectable at that. Well, then, the laundress. To her also Julie had likewise went. An' to her also Julie had passed the spondulicks. Now, I don't understand that so well, for laundresses don't overhear the ladies talkin', but, anyway, Julie told her if she wouldn't answer a question to anybody, she'd give her half a century, too. And did."

"Doubtless the laundress knew something Miss Van Allen wants kept secret."

"Doubtless, sir," said Fibsy, gravely.

"But I don't believe," mused Stone, "that it would help us any to learn all those women know. If Miss Van Allen thought they could help us find her, she would give them more than that for silence or get them out of the city altogether."

"Where is Miss Van Allen, Mr. Stone?"

Fibsy asked the question casually, as one expectant of an answer.

"She's in the city, Fibs, living as somebody else."

"Yep, that's so. Over on the West side, say, among the artist lady's studio gang?"

"Maybe so. But she has full freedom of action and goes about as she likes. Julie also. They come here whenever they choose, though I don't think they'll come while we're here. It's a queer state of things, Calhoun. What do you make of it?"

"I don't believe Vicky is disguised. Her personality is too pronounced and so is Julie's. I think some friend is caring for them. Not Ariadne Gale, of that I'm sure. But it may be Mrs. Reeves. She is very fond of Vicky and is clever enough to hide the girl all this time."

"The police have searched her house—"

"I know, but Mrs. Reeves and Vicky could connive a plan that would hoodwink the police, I'm pretty certain."

"I'll look into that," and Stone made a note of it. "About that carving knife, Fibsy. Did the caterers take it away by mistake?"

"No, sir; I 'vestergated that, an' they didn't."

"That knife is an important thing, to my mind," the detective went on.

"Yes, sir," eagerly agreed Fibsy. "It may yet cut the Gorgian knot! Why, Mr. Stone, the sewing lady knew that knife. She was here to lunching a few days before the moider, an' she says she always sat at the table in the dining room to eat, after Miss Van Allen got through. An' she says that knife was there, 'cos they had steak, an' she used it herself. I described the fork puffeckly, an' she reckernized it at onct."

"You're a bright boy!" I exclaimed in involuntary tribute to this clever bit of work.

"I'm 'ssociated with Mr. Stone," said Fibsy, with a quiet twinkle.

"It was clever," agreed Stone. "I'm sure, myself, that the absence of that small carving knife means something, but I can't fit it in yet."

We went up to the dining-room to look again at the carving fork, still in its place on the sideboard. I was always thrilled at a return to this room—always reminded of the awful tableau I had seen there.

The long, slender fork lay in its place. Though it had been repeatedly examined and puzzled over, it had been carefully replaced.

"But I can't see," I offered, "why a carving-knife should figure in the matter at all when the crime was committed with the little boning-knife."

"That's why the missing carving-knife ought to be a clue," said Stone, "because its connection with the case is inexplicable. Now, where is that knife? Fibsy, where is it?"

Fleming Stone's frequent appeals to the boy were often in a half-bantering tone, and yet, rather often, Terence returned an opinion or a bit of conjecture that turned Stone's cogitations in a fresh direction.

"You see, sir," he said, this time, "that knife is in this house. It's gotter be. That lady left the house in a mighty hurry but all the same she didn't go out a brandishin' of a carvin'-knife! Nor did she take it along an drop it in the street or an ash can for it'd been found. So, she siccreted it summer, an' it's still in the house—unless—yes, unless she has taken it away since. You know, Mr. Stone, the Van Allen has been in this house more times than you'd think for. Yes, sir, she has."

"How do you know?"

"Lots o' ways. Frinst' on Sat'day, I noticed a clean squarish place in the dust on a table in the lady's bedroom, an' it's where a book was. That book disappeared durin' Friday night. I don't remember seein' the book, I didn't notice it, to know what book it was, but the clean place in the dust couldn't get there no other way. Well, all is, it shows Miss Vick comes an' goes pretty much as she likes—or did till you'n me camped out here."

"Then you think she left the knife here that night, and has since returned and taken it away?"

"I donno," Fibsy scowled in his effort to deduce the truth. "Let's look!"

He darted from the room and up the stairs. Stone rose to follow.

"That boy is uncanny at times," he said, seriously. "I'm only too glad to follow his intuitions, and not seldom; he's all right."

We went upstairs, and then on up to the next floor. Fibsy was in Vicky Van's dressing room, staring about him. He stood in the middle of the floor, his hands in his pockets, wheeling round on one heel.

"They say she ran upstairs 'fore she flew the coop," he murmured, not looking at us. "That Miss Weldon said that. Well, if she did, she natchelly came up here for a cloak an' bonnet. I'll never believe that level-headed young person went out into the cold woild in her glad rags, an' no coverin'. Well, then, say, she lef' that knife here, locked up good an' plenty. Where—where, I say, would she siccrete it?"

He glared round the room, as if trying to wrest the secret from its inanimate contents.

"Mr. Stone says that walls have tongues. I believe it, an' I know these walls are jest yellin' the truth at me, an' yet, I'm so soul-deef I can't make out their lingo! Well, let's make a stab at it. Mr. Stone, I'll lay you that knife is in some drawer or cubbid in this here very room."

"Maybe, Fibsy," said Stone, cheerfully. "Where shall we look first?"

"All over." And Fibsy darted to a wardrobe and began feeling among the gowns and wraps hanging there. With a touch as light as a pickpocket's he slid his lightning-like fingers through the folds of silk and tulle, and turned back with a disappointed air.

"Frisked the whole pack; nothin' doin'," he grumbled. "But don't give up the ship."

We didn't. Having something definite to do, we did it thoroughly, and two men and a boy fingered every one of Vicky Van's available belongings in an amazingly short space of time.

"Now for this chest," said Fibsy, indicating a large low box on rollers that he pulled out from under the couch.

It was locked, but Stone picked it open, and threw back the cover. At the bottom of it, beneath several other gowns, we found the costume Vicky had worn the night of the murder!

"My good land!" ejaculated Fibsy, "the gold-fringed rig! Ain't it classy!"

Stone lifted out the dress, heavy with its weight of gold beads, and held it up to view. On the flounces were stains of blood! And from the wrinkled folds fell, with a clatter to the floor, the missing carving-knife!

I stooped to pick up the knife.

"'Scuse me, Mr. Calhoun," cried Fibsy, grasping my hand, "don't touch it! Finger prints, you know!"

"Right, boy!" and Stone nodded, approvingly. "Pick it up, Fibsy."

"Yessir," and taking from his pocket a pair of peculiar shaped tongs, Terence carefully lifted the knife and laid it on the glass-topped dressing table.

"Probly all smudged anyway," he muttered, squinting closely at the knife. "But there's sure some marks on it! Gee, Mr. Stone, there's sumpum doin'!" His eyes shone and his skinny little fingers trembled with excitement of the chase.

Stone studied the gold-fringed dress. The blood stains on the flounces, though dried and brown, were unmistakable.

"Wonderful woman!" he exclaimed. "Now, we've got this dress, and what of it? She put it here, not caring whether we got it or not. She's gone for good. She'll never be taken. This proves it to my mind"

"And the knife?" I asked, thrilling with interest.

"There you are again. If Miss Van Allen put that there for us to discover, the marks on it are of no use. Perhaps some she had put there purposely. You see, I'm inclined to grant her any degree of cleverness from what I know of her ability so far. She is a witch. She can hoodwink anybody."

"Except F. Stone, Esquire," amended Fibsy. "You pussieve, Mr. Calhoun, the far-famed detective, is already onto her coives!"

Stone looked up to smile at the boy's speech, but he returned his gaze to the golden-trimmed gown.

"Of course," he said, "it is improbable that she took this off before she left the house that night. I opine she threw a big cloak round her and rushed out to the house of some friend. Likely she found a taxicab or even commandeered some waiting private car for her flight. You know, we are dealing with no ordinary criminal. Now, if I am right, she brought this gown back here on some of her subsequent trips. As to the knife, I don't know. I see no explanation as yet. Since she stabbed her victim with another knife—why in the world hide this one up here? What say, Fibsy?"

"'Way past me. Maybe she was usin' both knives, an' the other one turned the trick, an' when she got up here she seen she had this one still in her grip, an' she slung it in this here chest to hide it. I ain't sure that's the c'reck answer, but it'll do temp'rar'ly. I say, Mr. Stone, I got an awful funny thing to ask you."

"It won't be the first funny thing you've asked me, Terence. What is it?"

"Well, it's pretty near eatin' time, an'—aw, pshaw, I jest can't dare to say it."

"Go ahead, old chap, I can't do more than annihilate you."

"Well, I wanna go to the Schuylerses to dinner."

"To dinner!"

"Yes, sir. An' not to the kitchen eats, neither. I wanta set up to their gran' table with their butlerses an' feetmen, an' be a nonnerd guest. Kin I, Mr. Stone? Say, kinni?"

Fleming Stone looked at the eager, flushed face. He knew and I did, too, that there was something back of this request. But it couldn't be anything of vital importance to our mystery.

"Oh, I understand," said Stone, suddenly. "You've taken a desperate fancy to Mrs. Schuyler and you want to further the acquaintance. But it isn't often done that way, my boy."

"Aw, now, don't kid me, Mr. Stone. Either lemme go or shut down on it, one o' the six! But it's most nessary, I do assure you."

"Maybe she won't have you. Why should those grand ladies allow a boy of your age at their dinner-table?"

"Because you ask 'em, sir." Fibsy's tone was full of a quiet dignity.

"Very well, I'll ask them," and Stone went away to the telephone.

Fibsy stood, looking raptly at the gold gown, and now and then his eyes turned toward the knife on the dressing-table. The table was covered with silver toilet implements, and save for its unfitting suggestion, the knife was unnoticeable among the other trinkets.

"It's all right," said Stone, returning. "Mrs. Schuyler sends a cordial invitation for all three of us to dine with her."

"Much obliged, I'll be there," said Fibsy, unsmilingly.

CHAPTER 18: FIBSY DINES OUT

That dinner at Ruth Schuyler's was memorable. And, yet, it was in no way markedly unusual. The service was perfect, as might be expected in that well-ordered household, and the guests were well behaved. Fibsy, thanks to Fleming Stone's thoughtful kindness, was arrayed in the proper dinner garb of a schoolboy, and his immaculate linen and correct jacket seemed to invest him in a mantle of politeness that sat well on his youthful buoyancy and enthusiasm.

I glanced round the table. It was a strange combination of people. Fleming Stone was the sort of man who is at ease anywhere, and I, too, am adaptable by nature. But the Schuyler sisters were very evidently annoyed at the idea of receiving as an equal the youth whom they regarded as a mere street arab.

Fibsy had become a firm friend of Ruth's, but he couldn't seem to like the other ladies, and he with difficulty refrained from showing this.

The Misses Schuyler were impressive in their heavy and elaborate mourning, and to my mind Ruth looked far more appropriately dressed.

She wore a black and white striped chiffon, with touches of black silk, and the effect, with her pale face and fair hair was lovely. A breastknot of valley lilies added to the loveliness, and I allowed my eyes to feast on her fairness. I had thought Ruth was not what could be called a pretty woman, certainly she was not beautiful; but that night her charm appealed to me more strongly than ever, and I concluded that her air of high-bred delicacy and infinite fineness were more to be desired than mere beauty.

Fibsy, too, devoured her with his eyes, though discreetly, and when he thought he was not observed.

Fleming Stone devoted himself to the sisters; probably, I concluded, because he was in their employ, and so owed them his attention.

Ruth wore her beautiful pearls, and referred to the fact, half-apologetically, saying that Mr. Schuyler had liked always to see them on her, and she felt privileged to continue to use them, even in her mourning period.

"You like only poils—pearls, don't you, Mrs. Schuyler?"

Fibsy's slip of pronunciation was due to his slight embarrassment at his novel surroundings, but he valiantly corrected himself and ignored it.

"I like other gems," Ruth replied, "but Mr. Schuyler preferred pearls, and gave me such beauties that I have grown very fond of them."

"I remember, Ruth," said Sarah, reminiscently, "how you used to beg Randolph for sapphires and diamonds instead. You even wanted semi-precious stones— turquoises and topaz. Oh, I remember. But Randolph taught you that pearls were the best taste for a young matron and you grudgingly acquiesced."

"Oh, not grudgingly, Sarah," and Ruth flushed at the reprimand in her sister's voice.

"Yes, grudgingly. Even unwillingly. In fact, all Randolph's decisions you fought until he made you surrender. You know how you wanted gay-colored gowns until he made you see that grays and mauves were better taste."

"Never mind my peccadilloes," said Ruth, lightly. "Let's talk of something less personal."

"Let's talk about the weather," suggested Fibsy, who was not conducting himself on the seen and not heard plan. "The park is fine now. All full o' red an' gold autumn leaves. Have you noticed it, Mrs. Schuyler?"

"Not especially," and Ruth smiled at him, in appreciation of his conversational help. "I must walk over there to-morrow."

"Yes,'m. An' why don't you go for a long motor; ride up Westchester way? The scenery's great!"

"How do you know, have you been there?"

"Not just lately, but I was last fall. Do you remember the big trees just at the turn of the road by—"

But Ruth was not listening to the child. Stone had said something that claimed her attention.

However, Fibsy was unabashed. With no trace of forwardness, but with due belief in his security of position as a guest, he continued to chatter to Ruth, and rarely addressed any one else.

He has something up his sleeve, I thought, for I was beginning to have great faith in the lad's cleverness.

He sat at Ruth's left hand, Stone being in the seat of the honor guest, and as that left me between the two sisters, I was doomed to participate in their chatter. But I was opposite my hostess and could enjoy looking at her in the intervals of conversation.

Suddenly, I chanced to look up and I saw Fibsy's comical little face drawn with grimaces as he sang a snatch of a popular song.

My heart goes twirly-whirly When I see my pearlie girlie,   With her—

"Now, what is that next line? With her—?"

"With her ring-around-a-rosy curls!" supplemented Ruth, her own face breaking into laughter, as, caught by the infection of Fibsy's waggish gayety, she rounded out the phrase.

"Yes, that's it" said Fibsy, eagerly, "and

Her teeth like little shining pearls,   Oh, she's my queen of all the girls,   My little twirly-whirly, pearlie Girlie!"

Ruth and Fibsy finished the silly little song in concert, and Stone clapped his hands in applause.

Rhoda sniffed and Sarah acidly remarked:

"How can you, Ruth? I wish you'd be a little more dignified."

Quickly the light went out of Ruth's eyes. She looked reproved, and though she didn't resent it, a patient sadness came into her eyes, and I resolved that I would do all I could to get it arranged that she should live apart from the two carping, criticizing sisters.

After dinner we had coffee in the library. Again, Fleming Stone took it upon himself to entertain the Misses Schuyler, and I drifted toward Ruth. She sat down on a sofa and motioned Fibsy to sit beside her. I drew a chair up to them and thanked a kind fate that let us all leave the table at once, dispensing with a more formal tarrying of the men.

After the coffee there were liqueurs. I glanced at Fibsy to see if he accepted a tiny glass from the butler's tray.

He did, and, moreover, he examined the contents with the air of a connoisseur.

"Oo de vee de Dantzic," he remarked, holding up his glass and gazing at the gold flecks in it.

We all smiled at him.

"Your favorite cordial, Terence?" asked Stone, affably.

"Yessir. Don't you love it, Mrs. Schuyler?"

"Yes," she said, and then, "why, no, I don't love it, child. But one gets accustomed to something of the sort."

"But don't you like it better than Cream de mint or Benediction?" he persisted.

Ruth laughed outright. "How do you know those names, you funny boy," she said.

"Read 'em on the big signboards," he returned. "They have the biggest billboards in New York for one of these lickures. I forget which one."

"These are what I like," said Ruth, smiling, as the footman passed a small bowl of sugared rose-leaves and crisp green candied mint leaves. "Take some, Terence. They're better for you than liqueurs. Help yourself."

"They are good," and Fibsy obeyed her. "They taste like goin' into a florist's shop."

"So they do," agreed Ruth, herself taking a goodly portion.

"Rubbish," said Rhoda. "I think these things are silly. Randolph would never allow them."

"Now, Rhoda, there's no harm in a few candies," protested Ruth, and then she changed the subject quickly, for she evaded a passage at arms with the sisters whenever possible.

The talk, however, soon drifted to the never forgotten subject of the murder. The sisters mulled over all they had heard or learned during the day and begged Stone to propound theories or make deductions therefrom.

Stone obeyed, as that was what he was employed for.

"I think Miss Van Allen is masquerading as somebody else," he affirmed. "I believe she is in some house not very far from this neighborhood, under the care of some friend and accompanied and looked after by her maid Julie. I believe she is in touch with all that goes on, not only from the newspapers but by means of some spy system or secret investigation. But the net is drawing round her. I cannot say just how, but I feel sure that we shall yet get her. It was a grievous mischance that I let her escape last night, but I shall have another chance at her, I'm sure."

"And then you'll arrest her," said Rhoda, with a snap of her thin lips.

"I dare say. Lowney tells me the finger prints on the little knife with which Mr. Schuyler was killed are clear and unmistakable, but we have not yet found out whose they are."

"And can you?" said Ruth, anxiously.

"If we find Miss Van Allen," said Stone, "we can at least see if they are her's."

"Pooh!" said Fibsy contemptuously, "why did'n' youse tell me before that you had the claw prints? I kin get Miss Van Allen's all right, all right!"

"How?" said I, for Fibsy had lapsed into the careless speech that meant business.

"Over to her house. Why, they're all over. I've only gotto photygraph some brushes an' things on her dressin' table to get all the prints you want."

"That's true," agreed Stone. "But it won't give us what we want. Nobody doubts that Miss Van Allen held the knife that stabbed Mr. Schuyler, and to prove it would be a certain satisfaction. But what we want is the woman herself."

It was then that I noticed Ruth's maid, Tibbetts, hovering in the hall outside the library door.

"You may go home, Tibbetts," Ruth said to her, kindly. "These gentlemen will stay late and I'll look after them myself."

Tibbetts went away, and Ruth said, explanatorily, "My maid is a treasure. I'd like to have her live here, but she is devoted to her own little roof tree and I let her off whenever possible."

I knew Tibbets had a home over on Second or Third Avenue, and I thought it kind of Ruth to indulge her in this. But after a change of domicile herself perhaps Ruth would arrange differently for her maid. And, too, as Winnie had often told me of Ruth's cleverness and efficiency in looking after herself and her belongings, I well knew she could get along without a maid whenever necessary.

"Did you ever trace that picture in Mr. Schuyler's watch?" Ruth asked, a few moments later.

"Yes," I said. "It was just as we supposed. A little vaudeville actress whom Mr. Schuyler had taken out to supper gave it to him, and he stuck it in his watch case, temporarily. Her name is Dotty Fay and she seemed to know little about Mr. Schuyler and cared less. Merely the toy of an evening, she was to him, and merely a chance that the picture was in his watch the night of his visit to Vicky Van's."

We had come to discuss the personal matters of Randolph Schuyler thus freely, for we were all at one in our search for the truth, and there were no secrets or evasions among us.

Ruth sighed, but I knew her dear face so well now that I realized it was not from personal sorrow, but a general regret that a man of Schuyler's ability and power should have been such a weakling, morally. I knew she had never loved her husband, but she had been a faithful and dutiful wife, and no word or hint of blame had ever escaped her lips regarding him. She had been a martyr, but I hadn't learned this from her. The sisters, though unconsciously, told me much of the deprivation and narrowness of Ruth's life. Schuyler had ruled her with a rod of iron, and she had never rebelled, though at times her patience was nearly worn out.

Later in the evening Fibsy asked for some phonograph music, expressing his great delight in hearing a really fine instrument and good records.

"I doubt if you'll care for our selections," Ruth remarked, as she looked over the cabinet of records. "They're almost all classical or old-fashioned songs."

"I like the classical kind," Fibsy said, endeavoring to be agreeable. "Please play the gayest you have, though."

But there were few "gay" ones in the collection. Wagner's operas and Beethoven's solemn marches gave forth their noble numbers and Fibsy sat, politely listening.

"No ragtime, I s'pose?" he said, after a particularly depressing fugue resounded its last echoes.

"No," and Ruth glanced at him." Mr. Schuyler didn't care for rag time—on the phonograph," she added, perhaps remembering Dotty Fay.

We stayed late. Several times Stone proposed our departure, but Ruth urged us to remain longer or began some subject of interest that held us in spite of ourselves. I had never seen her so entertaining. Indeed, I had never before seen her in what might be called a society setting. She was a charming hostess, and the occasion seemed to please her, for there was a pink flush on her cheeks and an added brightness to her gray eyes that convinced me anew of the joy she could take in simple pleasures.

She singled out Fibsy for her especial attentions, and the boy accepted the honor with a gentle grace that astounded me. When talking to her he lost entirely his slang and uncouth diction and behaved as to the manner born. He was chameleonic, I could see, and he unconsciously took color from his surroundings.

And sometimes I caught him gazing at Ruth with a strange expression that mingled amazement and sadness, and I couldn't understand it at all.

Again, I would find Ruth's eyes fixed on me with a beseeching glance that might mean anything or nothing.

As a whole the atmosphere seemed surcharged with a nameless excitement, almost a terror, as if something dire were impending. Once or twice I saw Stone and Terence exchange startled glances, but they rarely looked at each other.

There was something brewing, of that I was sure. But whatever it was it did not affect the Schuyler sisters. They were eager to talk, anxious to hear, but they felt nothing of the undercurrent of mysterious meaning that affected the rest of us.

I was glad when the time came to go. It was very late, nearly midnight, and I marveled to see that Ruth showed no sign of weariness. The sisters had been frankly yawning for some time, but Ruth's eyes were unnaturally bright, and her pale cheeks showed a tiny red spot on either side.

She shook hands nervously and her voice trembled as she said good-night.

Fleming Stone and the boy were moved, I could see that, but they made their adieux without reference to future meeting or further work on the mystery.

We went away, and as we turned the corner, I started to cross the street to go to my home.

"Come into the Van Allen house a few minutes, Calhoun," said Stone, gravely. "I've something to tell you."

We went in at Vicky Van's. Stone's manner was ominous. He and Fibsy both were silent and grave-looking.

We went in at the street door, into the hall and then to the living-room.

Stone and I sat down, and Fibsy darted out to the dining-room, back to the hall and up the stairs, flashing on lights as he went.

In silence Stone lighted a cigar and offered me one, which I took, feeling a strange notion that the end of the world was about to come.

In another moment Fibsy came slowly down stairs, walked into the living-room, where we were, gave one look at Stone, and then threw himself on a divan, buried his face in the cushions and burst into tears. His thin little frame shook with sobs, great, deep, heart-rending, nerve-racking sobs, that made my own heart stand still with fear.

What could it all mean? What ailed the boy?

"Tell me, Stone," I begged, "what is it? What has upset him so?"

"He has found Vicky Van," said Fleming Stone. "And it has broken his heart."

"What do you mean? Don't keep me in this suspense! Where is Vicky? Upstairs?"

"No," said Stone, "not now."

"Explain, please," I said, beginning to get angry.

"I will," said Stone.

"No!" cried Fibsy, "no, Mr. Stone, let me t-t-tell. W-wait a minute, I'll tell. Oh, oh, I knew it all day, b-b-but I couldn't believe it! I wouldn't believe it! Why, Mr.

Calhoun, Vicky Van is—is—why, Mrs. Schuyler is Vicky Van!"

CHAPTER 19: PROOFS AND MORE PROOFS

"You are absolutely crazy!" I said, laughing, though the laugh choked in my throat, as I looked at Stone. "You see, Fibsy, you're gone dotty over this thing, and you're running round in circles. I know both Mrs. Schuyler and Miss Van Allen, and they've nothing in common. There couldn't be two people more dissimilar."

"That's just it—that's how I know," wailed the boy. "That's how I first caught on. You see—oh, tell him, Mr. Stone."

"The boy is right," said Stone, slowly. "And the—"

"He can't be right! It's impossible!" I fairly shouted, as thoughts came flashing into my mind—dreadful thoughts, appalling thoughts!

Ruth Schuyler and Vicky Van one person! Why, then, Ruth killed—No! a thousand times NO! It couldn't be true! The boy was insane, and Stone was, too. I'd show them their own foolishness.

"Stop a minute, Stone," I said, trying to speak calmly. "You and the boy never knew Vicky Van. You never saw her, except as she ran along the street for a few steps at midnight. And Terence didn't see her then. It's too absurd, this theory of yours! But it startled me, when you sprung it. Now, Fibsy, stop your sobbing and tell me what makes you think this foolish thing, and I'll relieve your mind of any such ideas."

"I don't blame you, Mr. Calhoun," and Fibsy mopped his eyes with his wet handkerchief. He was a strange little figure, in his new clothes, but with his red hair tumbled and his eyes big and swollen with weeping. "I know you can't believe it, but you listen a bit, while I tell Mr. Stone some things. Then you'll see."

"Yes, Terence," said Stone; "go ahead. What about the prints?"

"They prove up," and Fibsy's woe increased afresh. "They ain't no shadder of doubt. The very reason I know they're the same is 'cause they're so unlike. Yes, I'll explain—wait a minute—"

Again a crying spell overwhelmed him, and we waited.

"Now," he said, regaining self-control, "now I've spilled all my tears I'll out with it. The first thing that struck me was the abserlute unlikeness of those two ladies. I mean in their tastes an' ways. Why, fer instance, an' I guess it was jest about the very first thing I noticed, was the magazines. In here, on Miss Van Allen's table, as you can see yourself, is—jest look at 'em! Vogue, Vanity Fair, Life, Cosmopolitan, an' lots of light-weight story magazines. In at Schuylers' house is Atlantic Monthly, Harper's, Century, The Forum, The North American Review, and a lot of other highbrow reading. An' it ain't only that the magazines in here are gayer an' lighter, an' in there heavier an' wiser; but there isn't a single duplicate! Now, Miss Vicky Van likes good readin', you can see from her books an' all, so why don't she take Harper's an' Century? 'Cause she has 'em in her other home—"

"But, wait, child," I cried, getting bewildered; "you don't mean Vicky Van lives sometimes in this house and sometimes in the Schuyler house as its mistress!"

"That's jest what I do mean. I know it sounds like I was batty, but let me tell more. Well, it seemed queer that there shouldn't be any one magazine took in both houses, but, of course, that wasn't no real proof. I only noticed it, an' it set me a thinkin'. Then I sized up their situations. Mrs. Schuyler's dignified an' quiet in her ways, simple in her dress, wears only poils, no other sparklers whatever. Vicky Van's gay of action, likes giddy rags, and adores gorgeous jewelry, even if it ain't the most realest kind. Now, wait—don't interrup' me, Lemme talk it out. 'Cause it's killin' me, an' I gotter get it over with. Well, all Mrs. Schuyler's things—furnicher, I mean—is big an' heavy an' massive, an' terrible expensive. Yes, I know her husband made her have it that way. But never mind that. Vicky Van's furnicher is all gay an' light an' pretty an' dainty colorin' and so forth. And the day the old sister-in-laws was in here they said, 'How Ruth would admire to have things like these! 'Member how she begged Randolph to do up her boodore in wicker an' pink silk?' That's what they said! Oh, well, I got a bug then that the two ladies I'm talkin' about was just the very oppositest I ever did see! Then, another thing was the records. The phonygraft in here is full of light opery and poplar music like that. Not a smell o' fugues and classic stuff. An' in at Schuyler's, as we seen to-night, there's no gay songs, no comic operas, no ragtime."

"But, Terence," I broke in, "that all proves nothing! The Schuylers don't care for ragtime and Vicky Van does. You mustn't distort those plain facts to fit your absurd theory!"

"Yes," he said, his eyes burning as they glared into mine. "An' Mr. Schuyler he wouldn't never let his wife go to the light operas or vodyville, an' she hadn't any records, so how—how, I ask you, comes it that she's so familiar with the song about 'My Pearlie Girlie' that she joined in the singin' of it with me at the dinner table to-night? That's what clinched it. Mrs. Schuyler, she knew that song's well as I did, and she picked it up where I left off and hummed it straight to the end—words and music! How'd she know it, I say?"

"Why, she might have picked that up anywhere. She goes to see friends, I've no doubt, who are not so straight-laced as the Schuylers, and they play light tunes for her."

"Not likely. I've run down her friends, and they're all old fogies like the sister dames or like old man Schuyler himself. The old ladies are nearly sixty and Mr. Schuyler was fifty odd, and all their friends are along about those ages, and Mrs. Schuyler, she ain't got any friends of her own age at all. But, as Vicky Van, she has friends of her own age, yes, an' her own tastes, an' her own ways of life an' livin.' An' she's got the record of 'My Pearlie Girlie.'"

"It's true, Calhoun," said Fleming Stone. "I know it's all incredible, but it's true. I couldn't believe it, myself, when Fibsy hinted it to me—for it's his find—to him belongs all the credit—"

"Credit!" I groaned. "Credit for fastening this lie, this base lie—oh, you are well named Fibsy!—on the best and loveliest woman that ever lived! For it is a lie! Not a word of truth in it. A distorted notion of a crazy brain! A—"

"Hold on, Calhoun," remonstrated Stone, and I dare say I was acting like a madman. "Listen to the rest of this more quietly or take your hat and go home."

Stone spoke firmly, but not angrily, and I sat still.

"Then, here's some more things," Fibsy continued. "I've gone over this house with a eye that sees more'n Mr. Stone's lens, an' it don't magnerfy, neither. I spotted a lot of stuff in the pantry and storeroom. It's all stuff that keeps, you know; little jugs an' pots of fine eatin'— imported table delicacies—that's what they call 'em. Well, an' among 'em was lickures an' things like that. And boxes of candied rose leaves an' salted nuts—oh, all them things. An' that's why I wanted to go to dinner at Mrs. Schuyler's an' see if she liked to eat those things. An' she did! She had the rose leaves an' she had the kind o' lickure that's down in the pantry cupboard in this house. An' she said it was her fav'rite, an' the old girls said she never used to have those things when her husband was runnin' the house—an' oh, dear, can't you see it all?"

"Yes, I see it," said Stone, but I still shook my head doggedly and angrily.

"I don't see it!" I declared. "There's nothing to all this but a pipe dream! Why shouldn't two women like Eau de vie de Dantzic as a liqueur? It's very fashionable—a sort of fad, just now."

"It ain't only this thing or that thing, Mr. Calhoun,"
said Fibsy, earnestly. "It's the pilin' up of all 'em. An' I
ain't through yet. Here's another point. Miss Van Allen,
she ain't got any pitchers of nature views—no landscapes
nor woodsy dells in this whole house. She jest likes
pitchers of people—pretty girls, an' old cavalier
gentlemen, an nymps, an' kiddy babies—but all human,
you know. Now, Mrs. Schuyler, she don't care anythin'
special for nature, neither. I piped up about the beauty
scenery out Westchester way an' over in the park, an' it
left her cold an' onintrusted. But she has portfolios of
world masterpieces, or whatever you call 'em, over to that
house, an' they're all figger pieces."

"And her writing desk," prompted Stone.

"Yessir, that checked up, too. You know, Mr. Calhoun,
they ain't nothin' more intim'tly pers'nal than a writin'
desk. Well, Miss Van Allen's has a certain make of pen,
an' a certain number and kind of pencils. An' Mrs.
Schuyler, she uses the same identical styles an'
numbers."

"And notepaper, I suppose," I flung back,
sarcastically.

"No, sir, but that helps prove. The note paper in the
two houses is teetumteetotally different! That was
planned to be different! Mrs. Schuyler's is a pale gray,
plain paper. Miss Van Allen's is light pink, to match her
boodore, I s'pose. An' it has that sort of indented frame
round it, that's extry fashionable, an' a wiggly gold
monogram, oh—quite a big one!"

I well remembered Vicky's stationery, and the boy
described it exactly,

"Proves nothing!" I said, contemptuously, but I
listened further.

"All right," Fibsy said, wearily pushing back his shock
of red hair. "Well, then, how's this? On Mrs. Schuyler's
desk the pen wiper is a fancy little contraption, but it's
clean-I mean it's never had a pen wiped on it. Miss Van

Allen's desk hasn't got any pen wiper. On each desk is a pencil sharpener, of the same sort. On each desk is a little pincushion, with the same size of tiny pins, like she was in the habit of pinnin' bills together or sumpum like that. On each desk the blotter is in the same place and is used the same way. There's a lot of pussonality 'bout the way folks use a blotter. Some uses both sides, some only one side. Some has their blotters all torn an' sorta nibbled round the edges, an' some has 'em neat and trim. Well, the blotters on these two desks is jest alike—"

"But, Fibsy," I cried in triumph, "I've seen the handwriting of these two ladies, over and over again, and they're not a bit alike!"

"I know it," and Fibsy nodded. "But, Mr. Calhoun, did you know that Miss Van Allen always writes with her left hand?"

"No, and I don't believe she does!"

"Yessir. I went to the bank an' they said so. An' I asked the sewin' woman, an' she said so. An' I asked the caterer people an' they said so. And the inkstand is on the left-hand side of Miss Van Allen's desk."

"All right, then she is left-handed, but that proves nothing!"

"No, sir, Miss Van Allen ain't left-handed. You know she ain't yourself. You'd 'a' noticed it if she had been. But she writes left-handed, 'cause if she didn't she'd write like Mrs. Schuyler!"

"Oh, rubbish!" I began, but Fleming Stone interrupted.

"Wait, Calhoun, don't fly to pieces. All Terence is saying is quite true. I vouch for it. Listen further."

"They ain't no use goin' further," said Fibsy, despondently. "Mr. Calhoun knows I'm right, only he can't bring himself to believe it, an' I don't blame him. Why, even now, he's sizin' up the case an' everything he thinks of proves it an' nothin' disproves it. But anyway, the prints prove it all."

"Prints?" I said, half dazedly.

"Yessir. I photographed a lot o' finger prints in both houses, an' the Headquarters people fixed 'em up for me, magnerfied 'em, you know, an' printed 'em on little cards, an' as you can see, they're all the same."

I glanced at the sheaf of cards the boy had and Fleming Stone took them to scrutinize.

"I got those prints from all sorts of places," Fibsy went on. "Off of the glass bottles and things in the bathrooms and off of the hair brushes and such things, an' off of the envelopes of letters, an' off the chairbacks an' any polished wood surfaces, an' I got lots of 'em in both houses, an' the police people picked out the best an' cleanest an' fixed 'em up, an' there you are!"

They seemed to think this settled the matter. But I would not be convinced. Of course, I'd been told dozens of times that no two people in the world have finger prints alike, but that didn't mean a thing to me. It might be, I told them, that Vicky Van and Ruth Schuyler were friends, that Ruth had withheld this fact, and that—

"No," said Stone, "not friends, but identical—the same woman. And, listen to this. Mrs. Schuyler heard us say this evening that Fibsy could photograph the brushes and such things over here to get Miss Van Allen's finger prints, and what does she do? She sends Tibbetts over to scrub and wipe off those same brushes, also the mirrors, chairbacks and all such possible evidence. A hopeless task—for the woman couldn't eradicate all the prints in the house. And, also, it was too late, for Fibsy had already done his camera work."

"How do you know she did all that?" and I glowered at the detective.

"Because Fibsy just told me he found evidences of this cleaning up, and, too, because Mrs. Schuyler purposely kept us over there longer than we intended to stay. You know how, when we proposed to say good-night, she urged us to stay longer. That was to give her maid more time for the work. Now, Mr. Calhoun, go on with your objections to our conclusions. It helps our theory to answer your refutations."

"Her letters," I mumbled, scarce able to formulate my teeming thoughts. "Vicky Van sent a letter to Ruth Schuyler—"

"Of course, she did. Wrote it herself, with her left hand, and mailed it to her other personality, in order to make the police give up the search. And, too, the letter from Miss Van Allen, found in Randolph Schuyler's desk after his death, was written and placed there by Mrs. Schuyler for us to find."

"Impossible!" I cried. "I won't allow these libels. You'll be saying next that Ruth Schuyler killed her husband!"

"She did," asserted Fleming Stone, gravely. "She did kill him, in her character as Vicky Van. Don't you see it all? Schuyler came here as Somers, never dreaming that Vicky Van was his own wife in disguise. Or, he may have suspected it, and may have come to verify his suspicion. Any way, when she saw and recognized him, whether he knew her or not, she lured him out to the dining room and stabbed him with the caterer's knife."

"Never!" I said. I was not ranting now, I was stunned by the revelations that were coming so thick and fast. I couldn't believe and yet I couldn't doubt. Of one thing I was certain, I would defend Ruth Schuyler to the end of time. I would defend her against Vicky Van—why, if Ruth was Vicky Van—where was this moil to end! I couldn't think coherently. But I suddenly realized that what they told me was true. I realized that all along there were things about Ruth that had reminded me of Vicky. I had never put this into words, never had really sensed it, but I saw now, looking back, that they had much in common.

Appearance! Ah, I hadn't yet thought of that.

"Why," I exclaimed, "the two are not in the least alike, physically!"

"Miss Van Allen wore a black wig," said Stone. "A most cleverly constructed one, and she rouged her cheeks, penciled her eyelashes and reddened her lips to produce the high coloring that marked her from Mrs. Schuyler."

I thought this over, dully. Yes, they were the same height and weight, they had the same slight figure, but it had never occurred to me to compare their physical effects. I was a bit near-sighted and I had never taken enough real personal interest in Vicky to learn to love her features as I had Ruth's.

"You see," Fleming Stone was saying, though I scarce listened, "you are the only person that I have been able to find who knows both Miss Van Allen and Mrs. Schuyler. No one else has testified who knows them both. So much depends on you."

"You'll get nothing from me!" I fairly shouted. "They're not the same woman at all. You're all wrong, you and your lying boy there!"

"Your vehemence stultifies your own words," said Stone, quietly; "it proves your own realization of the truth and your anger and fury at that realization. I don't blame you. I know your regard for Mrs. Schuyler, I know you have always been a friend of Miss Van Allen. It is not strange that one woman attracts you, since the other did. But you've got to face this thing, so be a man and look at it squarely. I'll help you all I can, but I assure you there's nothing to be gained by denial of the self-evident truth."

"But, man," I said, trying to be calm, "the whole thing is impossible! How could Mrs. Randolph Schuyler, a well-known society lady, live a double life and enact Miss Van Allen, a gay butterfly girl? How could she get from one house to the other unobserved? Why wouldn't her servants know of it, even if her family didn't? How could she hoodwink her husband, her sisters-in-law, and her friends? Why didn't people see her leaving one house and entering the other? Why wasn't she missed from one house when she was in the other?"

"All answerable questions," said Stone. "You know Miss Van Allen went away frequently on long trips, and was in and out of her home all the time. Here to-day and gone to-morrow, as every one testifies who knew her."

This was true enough. Vicky was never at home more than a few days at a time and then absent for a week or so. Where? In the Fifth Avenue house as Ruth Schuyler? Incredible! Preposterous! But as I began to believe at last, true.

"How?" I repeated; "how could she manage?"

"Walls have tongues," said Stone. "These walls and this house tell me all the story. That is, they tell me this wonderful woman did accomplish this seemingly impossible thing. They tell me how she accomplished it. But they do not tell me why."

"There's no question about the why," I returned. "If Ruth Schuyler did live two lives it's easily understood why. Because that brute of a man allowed her no gayety, no pleasure, no fun of any sort compatible with her youth and tastes. He let her do nothing, have nothing, save in the old, humdrum ways that appealed to his notion of propriety. But he himself was no Puritan! He ran his own gait, and, unknown to his wife and sisters, he was a roue and a rounder! Whatever Ruth Schuyler may have done, she was amply justified—-"

"Even in killing him?"

"She didn't kill him! Look here, Mr. Stone, even if all you've said is true, you haven't convicted her of murder yet. And you shan't! I'll protect that woman from the breath of scandal or slander—and that's what it is when you accuse her of killing that man! She never did it!"

"That remains to be seen," and Fleming Stone's deep gray eyes showed a sad apprehension. "But nothing can be done to-night. Can there, Terence?"

"No, Mr. Stone, not to-night. No, by no means, not to-night! It wouldn't do!" The boy's earnestness seemed to me out of all proportion to his simple statement, but I could stand no more and I went home, to spend the night in a dazed wonder, a furious disbelief, and finally an enforced conviction that Vicky Van and Ruth Schuyler were one and the same.

CHAPTER 20: THE TRUTH FROM RUTH

Next morning I was conscious of but one desire, to get to Ruth and tell her of my love and faith in her, and assure her of my protection and assistance whatever happened.

Whatever happened! The thought struck me like a knell. What could happen but her arrest and trial?

But as I went out of my own door—I left the house early, for I couldn't face Aunt Lucy and Winnie—I suddenly decided it would be better to see Stone first and learn if anything had transpired since I left him.

I rang the bell at Vicky Van's house with a terrible feeling of impending disaster, that might be worse than any yet known.

Fibsy let me in. I wanted to hate that boy and yet his very evident adoration of Ruth Schuyler made me love him. I knew all that he had discovered had been as iron entering his soul, but his duty led him on and he dared not pause or falter.

"We may as well tell him," he said to Stone, and the detective nodded.

"But come downstairs with us and have a cup of coffee first," Stone said; "you'll need it, as you say you've had no breakfast. Fibsy makes first-rate coffee, and I can tell you, Calhoun, you've a hard day before you."

"Have you learned anything further?" I managed to stammer out as we went down to the basement room that they used as a dining-room now.

"Yes; as I told you, walls have tongues, and the walls have given up the secret of how Mrs. Schuyler managed her two-sided existence."

But he would not tell me the secret until I had been fortified with two cups of steaming Mocha, which fully justified his praise of Fibsy's culinary prowess.

Fibsy himself said nothing beyond a brief "good morning," and the lad's eyes were red and his voice shook as he spoke.

"I knew," Stone said, as we finished breakfast, "that there must be some means, some secret means of communication between the two houses, the Schuyler house and this. You see, the Schuyler house, fronting on Fifth Avenue, three doors from the corner, runs back a hundred feet, and abuts on the rear rooms of this house, which runs back from the side street. In a word, the two houses form a right angle, and the back wall of the Schuyler house is directly against the side wall of the rear rooms of this house. Therefore, I felt sure there must be an entrance from one house to the other, not perceivable to an observer. And, of course, it must be in Mrs. Schuyler's own rooms; it couldn't be in their dining-room or halls. A few questions made me realize that Miss Van Allen's boudoir was separated from Mrs. Schuyler's bath room by only the partition wall of the houses. And I said that wall must speak to me. And it did."

We were now on our way upstairs, Stone ready at last to let me into the secret he had discovered.

We went to Vicky's boudoir, and he continued: "You know you found the strand of gilt beads caught in this mirror frame. We all assumed Miss Van Allen had flirted it there as she dressed for her party, but I reasoned that it might have caught there as she escaped to the Schuyler house the night of the murder. Yes, she did escape this way—look."

Stone touched a hidden spring and the mirror in the Florentine frame slid silently aside into the wall, leaving an aperture that without doubt led into the next house. The frame remained stationary, but the mirror slid away as a sliding door works, and so smoothly that there was absolutely no sound or jar.

I saw what was like a small closet, about two feet deep and perhaps three feet wide. At the back of it, that is, against the walls of the adjoining room in the other house, we could see the shape of a similar door, and the secret was out. There was no need to open that other door to know that it led to Ruth Schuyler's rooms. There was yet more telltale evidence. In the little cupboard between the houses was a small safe. This Stone had opened and in it was the black wig of Vicky Van and also a brown wig which I recognized at once as Julie's well-remembered plainly parted front hair.

"You see, Tibbetts is Julie," said Fibsy, in such a heart-broken and despairing voice that I felt the tears rush to my own eyes.

Vicky's wig! The loops of sleek black hair, the soft loose knot behind, the delicate part, all just as it crowned her little head—Ruth's head! Oh, I couldn't stand it! It was too fearful!

"This other door," Stone said, "opens into Mrs. Schuyler's bathroom. That I know. You see, she had to have this entrance from some room absolutely her own. Her bathroom was safe from interruption, and when she chose she slipped through from one house to the other and back at will."

"No, I can't understand it," I insisted, shaking my head. "If she came in here as Ruth Schuyler why wasn't she seen?"

"Because, before she was seen, she had made herself over into Victoria Van Allen. She had donned wig and make-up, safe from interruption, here in her boudoir. This make-up she removed before returning to the Schuyler house in her role of Mrs. Schuyler."

"It is too unbelievable!"

"No; it is diabolically clever, but quite understandable. Julie and Tibbetts are the same. This confidential woman looked after her mistress' safety on both sides. She remained when Vicky Van disappeared. She looked after everything, took care of details, attended to tradesmen and all such matters, and when ready followed Mrs. Schuyler into the other house, or went from here to her rooms a few blocks away and later came from them. When there were to be parties, Julie left the Schuyler house early, came here and made preparations, and then as late as ten or eleven o'clock maybe, Mrs. Schuyler came in from her home, when her own household thought her abed and asleep. She could go back in the early morning hours, with no one the wiser. Or, if she chose and she did when her husband was out of town, she could pretend she had gone away for a visit and stay here for days at a time."

I began to see. Truly the wall's tongue had spoken. If this awful theory of Stone's were true, it could only be managed in this way. I remembered how long and how often Vicky Van was absent from her home. I remembered that sometimes she was late in arriving at her own parties, although she always came down from upstairs in her party regalia.

"How did you come to suspect Tibbetts?" I asked, suddenly.

"Her teeth," said Fibsy. "I saw that Tibbetts had false teeth, anyway, an' I says, why can't Julie's gold teeth be false, too? And they are. They're in the safe!"

What marvelous precautions they had taken! To think of having a set of teeth for the maid Julie that should appear so different from those of Tibbetts! Surely this thing was the result of long and careful planning.

"Her glasses, too," went on Fibsy. "You see, they made her different from Tibbetts in appearance. That was all the disguise Tibbs had, the gold teeth, the big rimmed specs and the brown scratch—wig, you know. But it was enough. Nobody notices a servant closely, and these things altered her looks sufficient. Miss Van Allen, now, she had a wig an' a lot of colorin' matter an' her giddy clothes. Nothin' left to reckernize but her eyes, an' they were so darkened by the long dark lashes and brows that she fixed up that it made her eyes seem darker. I got all this from the pitchers the artist lady made. You see, she caught the color likeness but not the actual features. So I sized up the resemblance of the real women. Oh, Mr. Stone, what are we going to do?"

"Our duty, Terence."

Then I put forth my plea, that I might be allowed to go and see Ruth first; that I might prepare her for the disclosures they would make, the discoveries they would announce.

But Stone denied me. He said they would do or say nothing that would unnecessarily hurt her feelings, but they must accompany me. Indeed, he implied, that it might be as well for me not to go.

But I insisted on going, and we three went on our terrible errand.

Ruth received us in the library. She saw at once that her secret was known, and she took it calmly.

"You know," she said, quietly, to Stone. "I am sorry. I hoped to hide my secret and let Victoria Van Allen forever remain a mystery. But it cannot be. I admit all—"

"Wait, Ruth," I cried out. "Admit nothing until you are accused."

"I am accused," she responded, with a sad smile. "I heard you talking in the passage between the rooms. In my bathroom I could hear you distinctly. There is there a mirror door also. It looks like an ordinary mirror and has a wide, flat nickel frame, matching the other fittings. Yes, I had the sliding doors built for the purposes which you have surmised. Shall I tell you my story?"

"Yes, and let us hear it, too," came from the doorway, and the two sisters appeared, agog with excitement and curiosity.

"Come in," said Ruth, quietly. "Sit down, please, I want you to hear it. Most of it you know, Sarah and Rhoda, but I will tell it briefly to Mr. Stone, for I want not leniency, but justice."

I seated myself at Ruth's side, and though I said no
word I knew that she understood that my heart and life
were at her disposal and that whatever she might be
about to tell would not shake my love and devotion. It is
not necessary to use words when a life crisis occurs.

"I was an orphan," Ruth said, "brought up by a stern
and Puritanical old aunt in New England. I had no joy or
pleasures in my childhood or girlhood days. I ran away
from home to become an actress. Tibbetts, my old nurse,
who lived in the same village, followed me to keep an eye
on me and protect me in need. I was a chorus girl for just
one week when Randolph Schuyler discovered me and
offered to marry me if I would renounce the stage and
also gay life of any sort and become a dignified old-
fashioned matron. I willingly accepted. I was only
seventeen and knew nothing of the world or its ways. As
soon as we were married he forbade me any sort of
amusement or pleasure other than those practised by his
elderly sisters. I submitted and lived a life of slavery to
his whims and his cruelty for five years. He had agreed to
let me have Tibbetts for my maid, as he deemed her a
staid old woman who would not encourage me in
wayward desires. Nor did she. But she realized my
thraldom, my lonely, unhappy life, and knew that I was
pining away for want of the simple innocent pleasures
that my youth and light-hearted nature craved. I used to
beg and plead for permission to have a few young friends
or to be allowed to go to a few parties or plays. But Mr.
Schuyler kept me as secluded as any woman in a harem.
He gave me no liberty, no freedom in the slightest degree.

"I had been married about four years when I rebelled
and began to think up a scheme of a dual existence. I had
ample time in the long lonely hours to perfect my plans,
and I had them arranged to the minutest detail long
before I put them in operation. Why, I practised writing
with my left hand and acquired a different speaking voice
for a year before I needed such subterfuges. Had I been
able to persuade my husband to give me even a little

pleasure or happiness I would willingly have given up my wild scheme. But he wouldn't; so once when he was away on a long trip, I had the passage between the two houses made.

"I had previously bought the other house, under the name of Van Allen, for I had money of my own, left me by an uncle that Mr. Schuyler knew nothing about. Of course, this money came to me after I was married or I never should have wed Randolph Schuyler.

"Tibbetts' cousin, an expert carpenter, did the work, and, as he afterward went to England to live, I had no fear of discovery that way. Indeed, there was little fear of discovery in any way. I was expected to spend much of my time in my own rooms—and my bedroom, dressing room and bath form a little suite by themselves and can be locked off from the rest of the house. So, when I retired to my rooms for the night I could go through into the other house and become Vicky Van at my pleasure."

"I can't believe such baseness!" declared Rhoda Schuyler, "such ingratitude to a husband who was so good to you—"

"He wasn't good to me," said Ruth, quietly, "nor was I ungrateful. Randolph Schuyler spoiled my life; he denied me everything I asked for, every innocent pleasure and amusement. So, I found them for myself. I did nothing wrong. As Victoria Van Allen I had friends and pleasures that suited my age and my love of life, but there never was anything wrong or guilty in my house—"

"Until you killed your husband!" interrupted Sarah.

"Until the night of Randolph Schuyler's appearance at Vicky Van's house," Ruth went on. "I had been told of a Mr. Somers who wanted to know me, but I had no idea it was my husband masquerading under a false name. He came there with Mr. Steele. Of course, I recognized him, but he did not know me at once. I sat, playing bridge, and wondering how I could best make my escape. I saw that he didn't know me and then, suddenly as I sat, holding

my cards, and he stood beside me, he noticed a tiny scar
on my shoulder. He made that scar himself, one night,
when he hit me with a hot curling iron."

"What!" I cried, unable to repress an exclamation of
horror.

"Yes, I was curling my hair with the tongs and he
became angry at me for some trivial reason, as he often
did, and he snatched up the iron and hit my shoulder. It
made a deep burn and he was very sorry.

"Whenever he saw it afterward he said, 'Never again!'
meaning he would never strike me again. Then, when he
noticed the scar that night, although I had put on a light
scarf to cover it, he said 'Never again!' in that peculiar
intonation, and I knew then that he knew Victoria Van
Allen was his own wife.

"I ran out to the dining-room and he followed me."

"And you stabbed him!" cried Rhoda; "stabbed your
husband! Murderess!"

"I don't deny it," said Ruth, slowly. "The jury must
decide that. I must be tried, I suppose—"

"Don't, Ruth!" I cried, in agony. "Don't talk like that!
You shall not be tried! You didn't kill Schuyler! If you did
it was in self-defence. Wasn't it? Didn't he try to kill you?"

"Yes, he did. He snatched the little carver from the
sideboard and attacked me,—and I—and I—"

"Don't say it, Ruth—keep still!" I ordered, beside
myself with my whirling thoughts. The little carving-
knife!

"And you defended yourself with the caterer's knife—"
began Stone, but Fibsy wailed, "No! No! It wasn't Mrs.
Schuyler! I've got the prints from the caterer's knife and
they ain't Mrs. Schuyler's at all! She didn't kill him!"

"No, she didn't!" and Tibbetts appeared in the library
doorway. "I did it myself."

"That's right!" and Fibsy's eyes gleamed satisfaction;
"she did! It's her fingermarks on the knife that stabbed
old Schuyler. They're plain as print! Nobody thought of

matching up those marks with Tibbetts's mitt! But I'll bet she did it to save Mrs. Schuyler's life!"

"I did," and Tibbetts came into the room and stood facing us.

"Tell your story," said Stone, abruptly, as he looked at the white-faced woman.

"Here it is," and Tibbetts looked fondly at Ruth as the latter's piteous glance met hers. "I've loved and watched over Mrs. Schuyler all her life. I've protected her from her husband's brutality and helped her to bear his cruelty and unkindness. When she conceived the plan of the double life I helped her all I could, and I got my cousin to do the work on the houses that made it all possible. Then, I was Julie, and I devoted my life and energies to keeping the secret and allowing my mistress to have some pleasure out of her life. And she did." Tibbets looked affectionately, even proudly, at Ruth. "The hours she spent in that house as Victoria Van Allen were full of simple joys and happy occupation. She had the books and pictures and furniture that she craved. She had things to eat and things to wear that she wanted. She went to parties and she had parties; she went to the theatre and to the shops, and wherever she chose, without let or hindrance. It did my heart good to see her enjoy herself in those innocent ways.

"Then Mr. Schuyler came. I knew the man. I knew that he came because he had heard of the charm and beauty of Vicky Van. He had no idea he would find her his own wife! When he did discover it I knew he would kill her. Oh, I knew Randolph Schuyler! I knew nothing short of murder would satisfy the rage that possessed him at the discovery. I prepared for it. I got the little boning-knife from the pantry, and as Mr. Schuyler lifted the carver and aimed it at Ruth's breast I drove the little knife into his vile, wicked, murderer's heart. And I'm glad I did it! I glory in it! I saved Ruth's life and I rid the world of a scoundrel and a villain who had no right to live and breathe on God's earth! Now, you may take me and do with me as you will. I give myself up."

It was the truth. On the carving-knife appeared, plain as print, the finger marks of Randolph Schuyler, proved a hundred times by prints photographed from his own letters, toilet articles, and personal belongings in his own rooms. In his mad fury at the discovery of Ruth masquerading as Vicky Van, and in his sudden realization of all that it meant, he clutched the first weapon he saw, the little carver, to end her life and gratify his madness for revenge. Just in time, the watching Tibbets had intervened, stabbed Schuyler, and then ran upstairs, to escape through the hidden doors to the other house.

Ruth, stunned at the sight of the blow driven by Tibbetts, and dazed by her own narrow escape from a fearful death, picked up the carver that dropped from Schuyler's lifeless hand and ran upstairs, too.

She had, she explained afterward, a hazy idea that she was picking up the knife that Tibbetts had used, so bewildered was she at the swift turn of events. And as she stooped over Schuyler in her frenzy the waiter had seen her and assumed she was the murderer. This, too, explained the blood on the flounces of her gown—it had brushed the fallen figure of her husband and became stained at the touch.

The two women had, of course, slipped through the connecting mirror doors into the Schuyler house, and long before the alarm was brought there they were rehabilitated and ready to receive the news.

Then Ruth's quandary was a serious one. Innocent herself, she could not tell of her double life without making the whole affair public and incriminating Tibbetts, whom she loved almost as a mother and who had saved Ruth's life by a fraction of a second. An instant's delay and Schuyler's knife would have been driven into Ruth's heart.

So, for Tibbetts' sake, Ruth, perforce, kept the secret of Vicky Van.

"I was not ashamed of it," she told us, frankly. "There was nothing really wrong in my living two lives. My husband denied me the pleasure and joy that life owed me, so I found it for myself. I never had a friend or committed a deed or said a word as Victoria Van Allen that all the world mightn't hear or know of. And I should have owned up to the whole scheme at once except that it would bring out the knowledge of Tibbetts' act.

"I wished not to go back to the other house at all and should not have done so for myself. But I had reasons— connected with other people. A friend, whom I love, had asked the privilege of having certain letters sent her in my care, that is, in care of Miss Van Allen, and I had to go in once or twice to rescue those and so prevent a scandal that would ensue upon their discovery. For her sake I risked going back there at night. Also, I wanted my address book, for it has in it many addresses of people who are my charity beneficiaries. Mr. Schuyler never allowed me to contribute to any charitable cause, and I have enjoyed giving help to some who need and deserve it. These addresses I had to have, and I have them.

"Mr. Stone was right. The walls had tongues. He first noticed a little defect in the green paint in the living room, which I had retouched. Winnie told me of this, and I realized how clever Mr. Stone is. So, I threw away the paint I had used, which was in here, and I carefully thought out what else was incriminating and removed all I could from the other house. Fibsy noticed when I took a book from a table, but that book I wanted, because—" she blushed—"because Mr. Calhoun had given it to me and I wasn't sure I could get it any other way.

"But the walls told all, and at the last I knew it was only a question of time when Mr. Stone or Terence would discover the doors. I suppose the strand of beads that caught as I escaped that night gave a hint, but they would have found them anyway. They are wonderful doors—in their working, I mean. No complicated mechanism, but merely so well made and adjusted that a touch opens or closes them, and absolutely silently. No one in this house ever dreamed the bathroom mirror was anything but a mirror. And in the other house the elaborate Florentine frame precluded all idea of a secret contrivance. The two feet of thickness of the house walls made a tiny cupboard, where I had that small safe installed, that we might put our wigs and such definitely incriminating bits of evidence in hiding, also Vicky's jewelry. But I always changed my costumes from one character to the other in Vicky Van's dressing-room, and so ran little or no chance of discovery.

"In a futile endeavor to distract attention from Victoria Van Allen I wrote a note to Ruth Schuyler and also wrote the one found in Mr. Schuyler's desk. I did these things in hopes that the detectives would cease to watch for the return of Miss Van Allen, but it turned out differently. I assumed, of course, if search could be diverted from that house into other channels there would be a possibility of Tibbetts never being suspected. I am sorry she has confessed. I do not want her to be tried. She saved my life, and I would do anything to keep her from harm."

But Tibbetts was tried and was acquitted. A just jury, knowing all of the facts, declared it was a case of justifiable homicide, and the verdict was "Not guilty!"

The Schuyler sisters were finally convinced that Ruth's life had been endangered by their brother's rage, and, though they condemned Tibbetts in their hearts, they said little in the face of public opinion.

As for me, I couldn't wait until a conventional time had elapsed before telling my darling of my love for her own sweet self and, as I now realized, for Vicky Van also. I spent hours listening to the details of her double life; of the narrow escapes from discovery, and the frequent occasions of danger to her scheme. But Tibbetts' watchful eyes and Ruth's own cleverness had made the plan feasible for two years, and it was only because Ruth had found her dear heart was inclining too greatly toward me that she had begun to think it her duty to give up her double life. She had recently decided to do so, for she was not willing to let our mutual interest ripen into love while she was the wife of another man.

And so, if it hadn't all happened just as it did, I should never have won my darling, for she was about to give up the Van Allen house and I never should have had occasion to meet Mrs. Randolph Schuyler.

It is all past history now, and Ruth and I are striving to forget even the memories of it. We live in another city, and Tibbetts is our faithful and beloved housekeeper.

And often Ruth says to me: "I know you love me, Chet, but sometimes I can't help feeling a little jealous of the girl you cared for—that, what's her name? Oh, yes, Vicky Van!"

"Vicky Van was all right," I stoutly maintain. "I never knew a more charming, sweeter, prettier, dearer little girl than Vicky!"

"But she was awfully made up!"

"Yes, that's where you score an advantage. The only thing about Vicky I disapproved of was her paint and powder. Thank heaven, my wife has a complexion that's all her own." And I kissed the soft, pale cheek of my own Ruth.

THE END

Resurrected Press Mysteries From Louis Tracy

The Albert Gate Mystery
Four men murdered and a fortune in diamonds belonging to the Turkish Sultan stolen, while the Foreign Office official in charge has gone missing. Was it a common jewelry theft or was it a case of international intrigue? This is the question that barrister detective Reginald Brett must solve.

The Bartlett Mystery
When Ronald Tower is murdered on his way to a bridge game on the yacht Sans Souci it at first appears a common crime. But as Rex Carshaw finds, a tragic case of mistaken identity leads to political scandal among the rich and powerful of New York.

The Strange Case of Mortimer Fenley
When the wealthy Mortimer Fenley is struck down by a shot from an express rifle on the steps of his mansion, detectives Winter and Furneaux of Scotland Yard must find the culprit. Was it the artist who claimed he was painting a picture at the time of the shot? The disaffected younger son? Or is there another suspect?

The Stowmarket Mystery
For five generations the Fergus-Hume family has been cursed. Each of the baronets has met a violent end. When the fifth baronet is found slain by a ceremonial Japanese dagger, suspicion falls on his cousin David. It falls to barrister detective Reginald Brett to prove his innocence and find the real murder in a case that spans two continents and as many centuries.

Resurrected Press Mysteries by J. S. Fletcher

The Orange-Yellow Diamond
When an elderly pawnbroker is murdered in the London parish of Paddington, a young, down on his luck writer is accused of the crime. But then it's found the pawnbroker had had in his possession an extraordinary South African diamond worth over eighty-thousand pounds — a diamond that's now missing. It falls to Melky Rubenstein to unravel the mystery and prove the young man's innocence.

The Middle Temple Murder
When an elderly man's body is found on the steps of chambers in the Midde Temple, one of the Inns of Court, it falls to newspaperman Frank Spargo and Detective-Sergeant Rathbury to solve the crime. The murdered man, for indeed it was murder, was found with no money or identification on his person except for a piece of paper with the name and address of a young barrister. Who is the victim? Why was he killed? Who is the murderer?

Scarhaven Keep
Bassett Oliver, the famed actor, has gone missing. When Oliver fails to show for a rehearsal, aspiring playwright Richard Copplestone finds himself sent to the small village of Scarhaven on the northern coast of England to track down the actors movements. What he finds is mystery. Find the answers as Copplestone unravels the mystery of Scarhaven Keep.

Visit www.resurrectedpress.com

Resurrected Press Mysteries by Fergus Hume

The Green Mummy

Professor Braddock hoped to compare the burial practices of the Egyptians with those of the ancient Peruvians with his latest acquisition, the mummy of the last Inca, Caxas. But on arrival, the packing case proved to hold not the mummy, but the body of his assistant Sidney Bolton. It falls to Archie Hope to discover the murderer if he is to marry the professors step-daughter, Lucy Kendal. Who killed Bolton and where is the mummy? Was it the sea captain Hervey? The mysterious Don Pedro? Cockatoo the Polynesian servant? The professor, himself? And what has become of the emeralds? These are the questions that Hope must answer amongst the secrets of the past in The Green Mummy.

The Mystery of a Hansom Cab

"Truth is said to be stranger than fiction, and certainly the extraordinary murder which took place in Melbourne Friday morning goes a long way towards verifying that saying." Thus opens The Mystery of a Hansom Cab, the best selling mystery of the nineteenth century. When a man is found dead in a hansom cab one of Melbourne's leading citizens is accused of the murder. He pleads his innocence, yet refuses to give an alibi. It falls to a determined lawyer and an intrepid detective to find the truth, revealing long kept secrets along the way. Fergus Hume's first and perhaps most famous mystery... The Mystery Of A Hansom Cab.

Visit www.resurrectedpress.com

Resurrected Press Mysteries from the Dr. John Thorndyke Series

Dr. John Thorndyke - Lecturer on Medical Jurisprudence and Forensic Medicine. Before Bones, before CSI, before Quincy, M.E– there was Dr. John Thorndyke solving the most baffling cases of Edwardian London using the latest tools of medical science. Read about his cases in:

The Eye of Osiris
John Bellingham, noted Egyptologist has vanished not once but twice in the same day. Now Dr, Thorndyke must unravel the tangled claims on his estate, solve the riddle of the missing man and find the "Eye of Osiris".

The Mystery of 31 New Inn
When Dr. Jervis is whisked away in a coach with no windows to an unknown location to treat a man in a coma from undivulged causes it is Dr. Thorndyke who must come up with the solution.

The Red Thumb Mark
The first of Dr. Thorndyke's cases finds him trying to prove the innocence of a young man accused of being a diamond thief despite the fact that his finger print was found at the scene of the crime.

John Thorndyke's Cases
More cases of medical mysteries as told by his trusted assistant Jervis, M.D. Eight stories of crime and deduction in Edwardian London.

Visit www.resurrectedpress.com

Resurrected Press Mysteries by John R. Watson & Arthur J. Rees

The Hampstead Mystery

High Court Justice Sir Horace Fewbanks found shot dead in his Hampstead home, a butler with a criminal past, a scorned lover and a hint of scandal. These are the elements of the Hampstead Mystery that Detective Inspector Chippenfield of Scotland Yard must unravel with the assistance of the ambitious Detective Rolfe. But will he be able to sort out the tangled threads of this case and arrest the culprit before he is upstaged by the celebrated gentleman detective Crewe. Follow the details of this amazing case at it plays out across Hampstead, London and Scotland until it reaches a stunning conclusion in the courts of the Old Bailey.

The Mystery of the Downs

When Harry Marsland was caught in a sudden down pour he sought shelter at Cliff Farm. Met at the door by a young woman clearly expecting someone else he is only too glad to get inside to wait out the storm. When they hear a noise upstairs in the deserted house they investigate only to discover the body of the farm's owner, Frank Lumsden, dead of a gunshot wound. Who then, killed Lumsden, and why? Who was the woman expecting and did she have any roll in the murder? These are the questions that private detective Crewe must answer in The Mystery of the Downs.

Visit www.resurrectedpress.com

Other Resurrected Press Mysteries

Mysteries on a Train

Before the Orient Express there was:

The Rome Express by Arthur Griffiths
A man is found dead in his first class sleeping compartment on the express from Rome to Paris. Who was his murderer? The Countess? The English General? His brother the clergy man? The maid who has disappeared? Is the French justice system up to solving the crime? Read about it in The Rome Express.

The Passenger from Calais by Arthur Griffiths
Colonel Basil Annesley finds he is the only passenger on the train from Calais to Lucerne. That is until a mysterious woman shows up at the last minute to book a compartment. Who is after her? What is her secret? Is she a criminal or a victim? Read about it in The Passenger from Calais

Visit us at www.resurrectedpress.com

About Resurrected Press

A division of Intrepid Ink, LLC, Resurrected Press is dedicated to bringing high quality, vintage books back into publication. See our entire catalogue and find out more at www.ResurrectedPress.com.

About Intrepid Ink, LLC

Intrepid Ink, LLC provides full publishing services to authors of fiction and non-fiction books, eBooks and websites. From editing to formatting, from publishing to marketing, Intrepid Ink gets your creative works into the hands of the people who want to read them. Find out more at www.IntrepidInk.com.

www.ingramcontent.com/pod-product-compliance
Lightning Source LLC
Chambersburg PA
CBHW061133200626
46817CB00016B/1320